PIGS

PIGS

a novel

JOHANNA STOBEROCK

 Red Hen Press | *Pasadena, CA*

Book design by Mark E. Cull

Library of Congress Cataloging-in-Publication Data

Names: Stoberock, Johanna, author.
Title: Pigs : a novel / Johanna Stoberock.
Description: First Edition. | Pasadena, CA : Red Hen Press, [2019]
Identifiers: LCCN 2019017793 | ISBN 9781597090445
Subjects: LCSH: Pigs—Fiction. | Refuse and refuse disposal. | GSAFD:
Fantasy fiction.
Classification: LCC PS3619.T63 P54 2019 | DDC 813/.6—dc23
LC record available at https://lccn.loc.gov/2019017793

The National Endowment for the Arts, the Los Angeles County Arts Commission, the Ahmanson Foundation, the Dwight Stuart Youth Fund, the
Max Factor Family Foundation, the Pasadena Tournament of Roses Foundation, the Pasadena Arts & Culture Commission and the City of Pasadena
Cultural Affairs Division, the City of Los Angeles Department of Cultural
Affairs, the Audrey & Sydney Irmas Charitable Foundation, the Kinder
Morgan Foundation, the Meta & George Rosenberg Foundation, the Al-
lergan Foundation, the Riordan Foundation, Amazon Literary Partnership,
and the Mara W. Breech Foundation partially support Red Hen Press.

First Edition
Published by Red Hen Press
www.redhen.org

ACKNOWLEDGMENTS

Grateful and overwhelming thanks to Denise Shannon; to Kate Gale, Tobi Harper, Monica Fernandez, Rebeccah Sanhueza, Natasha Mc-Clellan, Tansica Sunkamaneevongse, Caitlin Sacks, Mark Cull, and everyone else at Red Hen; to Jessica Carballal, Martha Ives, David Ives, Peter Stoberock, and Denise Stoberock; to Dedi Felman, Fauzia Burke, Beth Parker, Shawn Wong, Liz George, Beth Hudson, Augusta Sparks Farnum, Manjushree Thapa, M Acuff, Julia Ireland, Claire Valente, Pat Sorenson, Katina Henderson, Debi Morehead, and Richele Loney; to the Jack Straw Foundation, Artist Trust, and the Whitman College Visiting Writers Reading Series; and to my family: Chris, Lucien, and Mila.

For Lucien, Mila, and Rebecca

The pigs ate everything. Kitchen scraps. Bitter lettuce from the garden. The stale and sticky contents of lunch boxes kids brought home from school. Toe nail clippings. Hair balls pulled up from the drain. After the pigs were done, there weren't even any teeth left over, not even any metal from cavities filled long ago.

They lived in a pen out back. The land was rocky but spacious, and the pen had been tucked in a corner out of sight for more years than any of the children could remember. It was made out of wood, gray splintered boards nailed together in a haphazard way. Every five feet, the wood was anchored by posts. When you stood by the fence, the pigs lumbered over, grunting, and stuck their snouts out between the rickety slats. It wasn't always that they expected food. Sometimes they just wanted their snouts scratched. Sometimes they just grunted happily and settled back down in the shade. There were six of them. They never fought. They seemed to smile when you approached. But you had to be quick. If you brought a bucket of slop and poured it out too slowly without moving your hand away, you never knew what could happen.

Luisa was missing a finger. Not an important one. Just her left hand pinky, where she hadn't moved away quickly enough one hot summer afternoon when she was feeding them shoes. It was summer every afternoon there. Soft and lazy and slow. The pinky came off in one clean bite before she even realized what was happening. She left with a feeling of shame, like it had been her fault the pig grabbed her finger. She wrapped her hand in her skirt and kept her mouth shut, and the stub didn't start hurting until she lay down for the night.

The land was actually an island. The island was surrounded by water that glinted green in the sun and clouded to gray in the shade. Some might have let the pigs run free, feral among the scrubby bushes. The pigs could have rooted happily for mushrooms or truffles, found entire brambles of berries to eat, and maybe left the children alone. They could have gobbled up the entire world's detritus without anyone's help. But the grown-ups preferred the pigs confined. They preferred the relative safety of the fence.

Luisa had lived on the island forever, or for as long as she could remember, which was the same as forever. There were other children too, three of them. Andrew, who sang in his sleep and had straw-colored hair. Mimi, who was older, or at least taller, than the rest, and who liked to pretend she knew much more about the world than anyone else, and who couldn't grow her hair long no matter how hard she tried. There was even a toddler. They called her Natasha. Her head was covered with loose blonde curls. She couldn't have been more than three, and she giggled every time she heard the grunting of the pigs.

They were all afraid of the gray water, of the sea in a mood of despair. It wrapped the island like a scarf made of grief. It made you choke with tears to touch it.

The children slept together in a whitewashed, one-room hut. They each had a space on the floor. It was comfortable and clean, and they were so used to each other that they never felt crowded. Mimi sometimes said she was getting older and needed more space, but the rest of them were happy to move over and let her have it. They didn't have beds, but they'd never heard of beds, and who needed beds anyway? They had blankets. They had pillows. They had mice that skittered along the edges of the room and ate breadcrumbs from the tips of their fingers.

The children ate fish for dinner every night. They picked berries and searched for bird eggs and kept watch from high rocks for sails and garbage on the horizon. Except for Luisa. The distance always blurred for her. Sometimes she wished she could get out on the water, get up close to those ships and find out where they came from. There was no way to tell from far away. But it was just a dream, and she never mentioned it to any of the others. Even in her head, she couldn't figure out how to make a seaworthy craft.

It didn't take long for Luisa's finger to heal into a nice, neat stump. She rubbed it sometimes, and whispered to herself that it was time to grow up and stop being clumsy. She tripped over things easily. She didn't notice roots or loose rocks or places where the earth buckled. She'd kick the ground in frustration and end up hurting her own foot. It was her fault she'd lost a finger. The pigs were fast, but if she'd been a little more agile they'd have snapped at air. She wondered what she'd tasted like. She hoped she'd tasted good, but not so good that the pig would want more. She tried to remember which one it was that had snapped at her, but even though she was pretty sure it was the one with black spots, she wasn't sure enough to say.

Sometimes the children tested what the pigs would eat. The leather flaps of shoe tongues. The bent frames of glasses. Mardi Gras beads. Tin cans. Pistols. Cap guns. There seemed to be no limit to their appetite. The children would stand a few feet away from the fence and toss whatever they were testing high into the air. The pigs moved with an un-expected grace, opening their long mouths and catching whatever came sailing down directly between their teeth. The pigs were remarkable. The children watched them with amazement, their own mouths open, their hands, now emp-ty, coming together of their own will to clap. Hub caps. The tassels off bicycle handlebars. Empty jars of mayonnaise. Gone, all gone in seconds.

The grown-ups on the island frowned at the children and never even pretended to help them with their chores. They drank espresso and smoked cigarettes and plugged their noses dramatically whenever the children got too close. As far as the children could tell, the grown-ups never cooked.

"It's not that they don't know how," Mimi said. She grabbed every opportunity to be the expert. "It's that they don't need to. Food appears. Why should they slave over a hot stove?"

"But what do they do?" Luisa said. "What do they talk about all day long?"

"Do they ever watch the pigs?" Andrew asked.

Natasha gulped and puffed out her toddler cheeks.

Nobody had the courage to ask. When Natasha fell into the gray water and came out covered in spots and filled with an unquenchable thirst for a parent that even Mimi couldn't solve, the grown-ups flinched at the sight of her.

"What are they here for?" Luisa said. Sometimes she thought, "Maybe we should just feed *them* to the pigs."

Ships passed by from time to time. Usually large cargo ships, but sometimes ocean liners. It was possible the island looked beautiful from a distance. When a ship edged onto the horizon, the children ran to the top of the highest rock and waved. They made Andrew take his shirt off, and Mimi circled it above her head. They didn't shout—they knew their voices weren't strong enough to carry all that way, and they didn't really want the grown-ups to hear them, not that the grown-ups had ever shown they'd cared. But this was private, and they'd agreed to do it in silence. Only once it seemed that they'd been sighted, but the only difference it made was that a barrel washed up on shore instead of the usual junk. They spent an entire day trying to pry it open, and when they finally got inside, all they found was another child. Sleeping.

His name was Eddie. If there had been a mirror, Luisa would have known immediately that he was her twin. As it was, she had to rely on the other children to tell her, and even then, she couldn't believe she looked anything like this pale, sleeping kid. His hands looked like they were made of wax. She couldn't imagine him ever doing work. It took him a long time to wake up. He didn't know how he'd gotten inside the barrel. He had a hard time remembering how to talk. He was even more afraid of the water than the rest of them, and when the pigs saw him, they went absolutely wild.

"Don't get too close," Luisa told him. "They think you're food. They don't know you yet. Stand back and throw this over the fence." She handed him a stale turkey sandwich, but instead of tossing it, he opened his mouth and took an enormous bite.

Mimi hit him hard across the head. "Are you crazy?" she said. "You don't eat what's meant for the pigs. My whole time here, I've never seen a kid stupid enough to do that. Spit it out. Spit it out right now and see if you can fix the idiot thing you've done." She held her hand out. He turned away from her and kept chewing.

The pigs were rushing back and forth, throwing themselves against the fence. Natasha started crying. Andrew picked apricots off the closest tree and threw them in to try to calm the pigs down. They jumped for the fruit, and it seemed they jumped higher than anyone had ever seen them jump before. They practically looked like ballet dancers. Any higher, and they'd be over the fence.

"Throw them the sandwich," Mimi said again. But Eddie stuffed the last piece in his mouth, turned his back to the pigs, and headed up the path to the hut.

When the other children got back, they found him trying to push the boards of the barrel back together. In their rush and difficulty to get it open, they had pulled out nails and splintered the wood. Now Eddie seemed to think, incorrectly, that there was some possibility of repair.

"You can't leave," Mimi said. "It doesn't work that way."

Luisa tried to speak more softly. After all, they told her he was her twin. "It's not so bad," she said. "I'll take you for a walk this afternoon. There are a lot of nice things to see. And you can tell us what it's like off the island. You can tell us what we're missing."

Eddie shrugged. He walked into the hut and curled up and went to sleep.

Luisa muttered under her breath that she'd been trying to be nice. She stamped her foot on the ground and yelped when she twisted an ankle.

The grown-ups were even less interested in the new boy than in the other children. They didn't seem to think he'd last. They glanced at him sideways, lit new cigarettes, reapplied lipstick, poured themselves martinis, and continued with their conversations.

"In Costa Rica, can you believe it?"

"An ecolodge? Are you kidding me? You should see her in shorts."

"They say nobody goes to Paris anymore."

"Who does? Paris is immortal."

Their talk was as constant a murmur as the lapping of waves from the ocean. Like the ocean, it often sparkled. And like the ocean, it had gray moments from which the children knew they must stay away.

"She said I looked fat."

"What should we do to her?"

"I haven't decided yet. But something."

When the tone shifted, the children knew to run.

There was a cave at the far end of the island. The children didn't think the grown-ups knew about it—why would they? The grown-ups never scurried through the underbrush. If they couldn't reach a place using carefree, elegant strides, they didn't go. It was a rule among the children not to wonder out loud about what the grown-ups did when the children were hiding in the cave. If they'd been brave enough to use their voices in the dark there, they might have said pedicures. Or maybe salsa classes. Or yoga. But hunting? The children might think it, but they would never let the words pass their lips. If they didn't say it, it probably couldn't be true.

The cave was long and narrow, black as a heart inside, cold and hollow and dense, and it offered shelter against the shifts in the outside world. A gray ocean? Head to the cave. A sea-change in tone? Head to the cave. A loose pig? It had never happened, but if it did, the cave seemed the best bet. The pigs probably wouldn't eat stone. They'd probably eat all of the island's vegetation before sinking their teeth into the boulder that the children had ready to roll across the opening. Each child had a space to sleep in the cave, the way they each had a space to sleep on the floor of the hut. They brought clay jugs filled with water and hid them in the darkest part. The grown-ups didn't notice the jugs were missing, and that made the children feel subversive and dirty, but it also made them feel safe.

"We need the water," Mimi said. "They're not going to help us if the pigs get loose. They must have some escape plan without us. If one of those pigs gets out, we'd be done without a plan."

So there it was: a cold dark security blanket hidden at the island's far end that they treasured as much as they treasured whatever other secrets were buried in each of their hearts. The grown-ups might control them. The grown-ups might sit back while they worked. The grown-ups might laugh when they were in pain. But the children had a plan. They had a shelter that they could hide in forever, if it came to that.

They couldn't decide what to tell Eddie about the cave. He didn't seem trustworthy. He didn't seem anything at all, actually, with his big silent sandwich-chewing mouth and his nose sprouting the first traces of acne and his hands that had clearly never done work in their life and his eyes that looked back at Luisa's with a gaze she hoped she didn't have herself. It was empty. She didn't feel empty. She felt as though everything she'd ever fed to the pigs had settled inside her as well. Maybe she wasn't seeing him accurately— every day the world seemed blurrier even than it had before. But it was hard to mistake emptiness, no matter how bad your vision.

It turned out that they never actually had to make a decision because Eddie made it for them. Three days after he arrived, on a gray, cloudy day, he took a long stick and carried it to the ocean and started poking at the water. He probably thought he was looking for crabs. He might have been watching ripples spread out in circles. Whatever it was, the sea didn't like it and Luisa, watching him secretly from not too far away, noticed tendrils twisting their way toward his hand. He was as oblivious to them as he was to everything else, and she had to run forward to stop him. She stumbled—it seemed like there were roots everywhere just waiting for her—but she righted herself and got to him in time. She knocked the stick away, grabbed his arm, and, before he could push her off, jerked him away from the water.

"You can't poke at the ocean," she said. "Look at the mood you've put it in." He didn't say anything in response. He never said anything. He just stared at her and then looked away. "You'll get a rash. Or something else. You should see Natasha's scars from the last time she touched it. And she wasn't even poking. She was just trying to play. Come on."

She pulled him and when he didn't move, she pulled him again harder. This time he pulled back, and then he pushed her off and she shoved him hard and he stumbled back and then his feet were in the water. Up to his ankles. Splashing up to his knees. The water gripped him and tried to pull him deeper. And he screamed. And his scream was louder than any scream Luisa had ever heard. And as soon as he screamed the water turned darker, and she heard a drum start beating up in the hills. The sea started heaving, gray and angry, and she screamed, too. The entire island seemed to hold its breath. Eddie's face was pale and his mouth twisted, and he struggled to get out of the water. His screams were steady now, like they'd never end, and Luisa splashed in herself and yanked him toward the sand.

Her wet legs burned. Her throat got tight. A sob pushed through her lips, but she sucked it back in and pulled and pulled until they both fell backward onto the sand, away from the water. The water, like tongues, licked just inches away. She'd pushed him in. What had she done? She couldn't hold the sobs back now.

A laugh carried down from the villa where the grown-ups lived. A laugh, and then a shriek.

"We have to run," she said.

Eddie looked at her. Red welts were forming on his legs. He leaned over and vomited.

"Run now," she said. "They're going hunting. We've got to go."

She dragged him by the arm and this time he followed, whimpering but moving fast.

The other kids were already in the cave by the time they got there. They helped Luisa push Eddie inside, and then, all together, they rolled the boulder across the opening. Darkness closed around them. Silence. They were used to it, and they didn't even try to whisper. They could wait it out. They'd waited it out before. The sun would come back out. The sea would turn bright blue again. The grown-ups would realize they all just needed a nap. Just be quiet, they all thought inside their heads. Just wait and don't make a sound.

Luisa's whole body ached, but she bit her lip and kept her mouth shut. Then, from nowhere, but really from Eddie, a moaning rose. It was like the wind. It was like the water. It was like a car that hadn't been started in a long time, whose engine wasn't sure it would ever turn again.

"Shut up," Mimi said.

"They'll hear us," Andrew said.

The moaning kept on.

"So your legs hurt," Luisa hissed. "Mine hurt too. It's your own fault, anyway. The water was clearly gray. You have to stay away from it when it's like that. If you hadn't been poking at it, we wouldn't be here. Shut up."

They couldn't silence him. In the dark, with all five crowded together, they couldn't figure out who was Eddie, and they kept slapping their hands across each other's mouths. They had no idea how long it went on until they heard a voice, exhuberant and adult, just outside the cave.

"By golly, I think I've found them," they heard.

"Not really? You've found the little scamps?"

"Do you hear that moaning? The new boy must not realize he's in hiding. What luck!"

Luisa shivered. Her finger throbbed. The languorous adult conversations were never supposed to directly involve them. They cowered toward the back of the cave and tried to turn to stone themselves.

"Roll back that rock," a voice said.

"But my nails. I've just had them done."

"Use this crowbar I happen to have with me."

"You're so handy."

"You're so lovely."

From just beyond the boulder came the sounds of kissing. The children felt a collective "ugghh" pass through them, but they knew control, and only Eddie made a sound. It was another moan, but they could translate it easily: "Let me go home," the moan said. "I want to go home."

Then came a scraping and some grunts of hard work, and then the stone rolled back.

Daylight invaded. The smell of thyme and lavender. The squeals, far away, of pigs. And then, blocking the light, platinum blonde hair pulled back, the scarlet-lipped face of one of the grown-ups appeared, smiling, teeth so white they might as well have been painted.

"I've got them," she sang. She reached her hand out quicker than a whip, pressing her nails into Luisa's upper arm. "Come out, darling." Luisa found herself hurled into the open air, into the light, into a giant net as if she were a butterfly. One by one she was joined by the other children, until even Eddie, no longer moaning but still crying, huddled in the light beside her.

"We've been searching for hours," the man said. His black hair was slicked back and his eyes were green. "Silly things. Did you think we wouldn't find you? The pigs need feeding. The ocean needs tending. It's sent us some more junk. You've been delinquent in your work."

"Look at them," the woman said. "They're scared, poor things. Let's get them back home where they can clean up and get some rest. Maybe an early bedtime tonight."

"Early to bed, early to rise," the man said.

"That's what I always say," the woman answered. They started laughing uncontrollably, and it was minutes until they calmed down enough to jab at the children with sticks.

It isn't easy walking in a net, especially across an unpaved island. There was a path, but it was narrow and encroached upon by thorn bushes. The woman walked ahead, her ankles twisting in her high heels from time to time. She looked elegant, but it was clear that she was in a certain amount of pain. She muttered curses under her breath. The man followed, prodding at the children occasionally with his crowbar. The children didn't speak, but Luisa held Mimi's hand, and Natasha clung to Mimi's leg, and even Eddie, whom they all blamed for the trouble, kept his hand on Andrew's arm. It was hot, and the air around them smelled too sweet, and halfway down the path Eddie started hiccupping. By the time they got back to the hut, they were covered in thorns and skinned knees and bleeding bottom lips, and nobody cared that Eddie had oozing red sores up and down his legs. Luisa had welts on her legs, too. They were all in pain. The grown-ups pushed the net, children and all, into a hollow just outside the hut, and left them there to go have something tall and cool.

The pigs were loud now. They grunted and snorted as if they were giggling. Luisa counted them in her mind—the one with the spots, the one with the lopped off ear, the one whose hooves looked dainty, the one who liked to scratch her side against the fence post, the one who was smaller and skinnier than the rest but who seemed to have the sharpest teeth of all, and the one she always forgot to count. She wondered which was talking. She wondered if they were dividing the children up among them. They wouldn't divide evenly—five into six. She wondered what the pigs would look like bathed and with wreathes of flowers around their necks.

Far, far along the horizon, a ship passed. It was hard to tell, but it was probably a cargo ship. An oil tanker, maybe. Just the kind to send some junk ashore that evening. Razor wire? Plastic table cloths? Leaky tents? Incorrect homework that no one had bothered to do over? Maybe the pigs would get a double meal. It didn't happen often, but when it did, it didn't seem to faze them. Pigs don't know when they're full. They can eat and eat and eat until their stomachs burst. A couple of children in the morning? A couple of sailors in the early afternoon? Some high heeled shoes for dessert? They'd do their best, or die trying.

"Mimi," Luisa said. "How old was I when I got here?"

"Her age." Mimi nodded toward Natasha. "Little and skinny and already tripping over your own feet."

"Where do you think I came from?"

"No idea. No idea where any of us are from."

"I know," Eddie said. They looked at him in surprise. They'd begun to think he didn't know how to use words. His voice was stronger than they would have thought. His eyes were the same brown as Luisa's, and his soft hands had the same crooked little fingers, but he seemed older now that he had a voice. "I was awake when they put me in the barrel."

"You were not," Mimi said. She kicked him. He yelped, and then he kicked her back. They scuffled briefly, but there wasn't much room for fighting inside the net.

"I was lying in my bed, fast asleep in the castle. Then something shook me. I thought it was my nurse, and I opened my eyes, but it was a man, and he said it was time to go. He said I was joining my sister, that I should have been sent away with her right from the start. He said that they should have known I'd break as many things as she did. He said they should have known I'd be just as much of a disaster. My sister." He looked at Luisa. Then he spat. "They blindfolded me, then they took me riding somewhere on a horse, and then we were on a ship, and then they stuffed me in a barrel, and then you found me."

"Why didn't you say anything before? Why did you make so much noise in the cave?"

"I was hurt," he said. "The ocean? My legs? Remember?"

"Kids on the island don't make noise," Andrew said. "We listen, and we feed the pigs, but we don't draw attention to ourselves. You messed up."

"I didn't mess up," Eddie said. "I was hurt. I'm allowed."

"What a jerk," Mimi said.

"Total jerk," Luisa said. A disaster. She shut her eyes and saw herself pushing him into the gray water. She wanted to kick him. If she hadn't pushed him, he probably wouldn't have screamed. If he hadn't screamed, who knew if the hunt would have started? So now they were in a net because of her. She couldn't do anything right. Her brother. He might look like her, but that was where the resemblance ended. She didn't even know what a brother was supposed to be.

"Nothing's going to happen," Eddie said. "We're kids."

Far away, the ship blew its horn. Night was coming. The garbage would wash up soon.

"How many fingers do you have?" Mimi asked.

"Ten," he said. "Why?"

"Count mine," she said. She held up her hands. Luisa had never really looked at Mimi's hands. She'd been so aware of her own lost finger that she never thought to see if others had lost fingers as well. Mimi was missing three. Two on her left hand—her pointer and her middle finger—and one on her right—her innocuous pinky, so small. Luisa knew from experience that the loss of a pinky didn't really make a difference, but a pointer?

"The thumb's the next to go," Mimi said. "What do you have to say about that?"

Eddie kept quiet. He looked at his hands, and then slowly began to clean his fingernails.

A breeze picked up. The wind was blowing toward them, salty air across rocks and through wild roses. The sun was low on the horizon. The ship had sailed beyond their line of vision. The grunting of the pigs had grown to a soft murmuring that blended in with the waves lapping across the rocks. The voices of the grown-ups carried down from their villa, the delicate clink of ice against glass, the laughter at some droll remark or another.

Eddie was shivering now. The other children looked at one another and rolled their eyes, but Luisa reached out and put her hand on his.

"I loved the castle," Eddie said. "My bedroom was in a tower, and it had a fireplace, and my bed had purple curtains that I could pull shut whenever I didn't want to see the maid. My mother and father came at night to tuck me in. I had a lamp that I could light to read by late, late into the night. Nobody ever came to tell me to turn it off. I was on my own as much as I wanted, and when I didn't want to be on my own, there was always someone there. I had books and a guitar and they were going to get me a phone for my next birthday. The ocean was a treat: a hot day, sandy, sit under an umbrella and occasionally go get an Italian ice treat. I don't like this net."

Luisa felt her face get hot and she pulled her hand away. She'd give anything to see a world like that up close. Purple curtains. Italian ice. She'd give anything to get off the island, even for a single day.

Mimi and Andrew nodded. Natasha, silent as always, put her little head on Mimi's knee. The pigs snorted, loud and impatient. They would be hungry in the morning. They would open their mouths for anything.

After Eddie fell asleep, the children looked at one another and rearranged themselves. Mimi settled into the far corner of the net, pulling Natasha in to cuddle with her. Andrew curled down by her feet. Luisa climbed silently over Eddie and nudged him until he lay between her and the net's opening. All four were huddled as far away from him as possible. He was her brother, but what difference would that make once the grown-ups returned? He had slept in a bed. He had read books. He knew what it was like to ride a horse. He was as much a sacrifice as anything the children had to offer. *Take him*, Luisa thought. *Take him. He's not one of us. Take him and do whatever it is that makes you happy.* She lay awake far into the night, listening to Eddie's breathing, hoping that when the grown-ups came, they came to untie the net with their hard nailed fingers instead of cutting it open with long knives. Either way, they'd pull the one closest to the opening out first. Either way, it would be Eddie and not her.

O tis couldn't stop crying even though he knew he was wasting whatever liquid his body had left. His eyes were full of sand. The tears washed the grit from his eyes, which was some consolation, but not enough. At least it restored vision, which after five days drifting on the lid of a packing crate at sea was a pretty big deal. If he lifted his head slightly from where it was wedged into the sand he could see the coast. Rocky. Dry. Dotted with bursts of purple flowers pushing out of cliffs. Maybe enough driftwood on the beach to build a shelter. There were birds—seagulls anyway. They stood in a line and looked at him. He could swear they were looking right at him. He thought he heard a dove.

Get up, he told himself. *Move. Take responsibility for your life. You're not a child. Nobody's going to take responsibility for you.*

He crawled away from the water, and his body left a long track behind him on the sand.

He had no idea how long it took to be able to stand up, but it happened. At one point his cheek was shoved against a rough pillow of sand and at the next he was standing with his knees shaking, the breeze from the ocean on his neck. Even though it had happened five seconds ago, he couldn't say how he'd gotten from one position to the other. Something rubbed against his throat. He lifted his hand and felt the smooth surface of a metal pendant. A necklace? He remembered he'd had a necklace. The chain was heavy against his battered skin.

He dragged driftwood into a pile. He hobbled to the place where the sand stopped and vegetation began. He listened and heard a stream, and bushwhacked through thorny bushes until he found fresh water. Then, he got back down on his knees and stuck his face in and drank. Alice had once washed his hair under the bathtub faucet when he'd had the flu and was too sick to climb into the tub. It felt like that now, head in the stream, water in his mouth—it felt like someone loved him.

He thought he could drink that water forever.

But before too long he started to shake again and he thought, *three hours without shelter, three days without water, three weeks without food.* Where did he know that from? Boy Scouts? Had he really ever been a boy? He'd learned the rule during some kind of wilderness training. Was this the wilderness? Somehow he'd always imagined wilderness to be about trees. *Shelter, water, food.* He cupped his palm and lifted water to his mouth and took another swallow and realized he was doing everything in the wrong order. As usual. He hobbled back through the brambles to the beach.

He had more energy now. At least the water had given him that. He should stay close to the ocean so if a ship passed by, he'd see it. He needed to build a fire so if a ship did pass by, and he did see it, he'd have some way of letting it know he was there. A voice at the back of his mind told him no one would care. He tried not to listen. He'd always tried not to listen to what people told him about himself. That voice had been telling him to let go the whole time he'd been floating in the ocean, and look how wrong it had been. Look where he was. He even had fresh water.

The line of gulls stared at him and one turned her head and her eyeball glittered and he noticed that the sun was sinking low. Night was on its way, and he was hungry. He couldn't decide what to do first. Shelter or food? Find more water or build a fire? There were too many choices; even the limited options were overwhelming. Life had always been that way for him. He'd never been able to make up his mind. He lifted his hand to the pendant at his throat and thought: *this is what I do when I think. I hold this pendant. This is who I am.* He fiddled with the pendant; found himself fumbling at a hinge. *Not a pendant*, he thought. *A locket. I hold this locket and I flip its catch open and closed until I can make a choice.*

He pulled the locket's door open. Alice stared out at him, a smile on her long mouth, her light brown hair pushed back behind her ears. She was young in the picture—in her twenties, maybe. She was wearing a flowered shirt. He remembered that shirt. He'd called her his flower child when she wore it. Across from Alice, their son stared out from years ago, round baby eyes not yet a real color, a blue hat on his bald head. Otis shut the door. He opened it again. He shut it and opened and shut it and opened it, trying to make a choice.

But there wasn't really a choice. The rule of threes: it had to be shelter, and soon. He shoved a couple sticks together to make a kind of lean-to. It had gaps, but if he scooted his body inside, his head was covered and only his legs were exposed to the wind that was kicking up now from the water. He could sort of see the stars through the gaps when night really fell. The stars here were just as bright as they'd been when he'd clung to wood in the middle of the ocean, just as bright, if not brighter.

He couldn't even tell himself how tired he was with that voice that chattered constantly in the back of his head—

was it really telling him that his clothes were ruined? Was it really telling him he should have spent more hours at the gym? Really? Lying there, half-sheltered, half-exposed, he had the feeling of sinking into the ground. He used a nail he'd pulled from the crate in the ocean to notch a line into a board above him. A first day.

He fell asleep trying to remember methods for making fire without a match. Flint. Hand drill. Bow drill. Magnifying glass. There had to be other ways, he just couldn't remember. The locket was cold on his skin.

From a distance, the island looked so small that ocean liners moving past described it to their passengers as nothing but an unnamed, uncharted outcropping of rock. Cruise directors announced over loudspeakers that some people said it was the island where the sirens tried to lure sailors to their death. Listen closely, they said, and you'll hear something that sounds like a song. From time to time, a half-drunk divorcee jumped into the water and required rescue from irritated sailors. From time to time passengers gathered on deck to sigh at the dark outline the island made against the orange setting sun. But nobody noticed the trails of refuse that formed a path over the water as the ship steamed on. It was official policy never to look back. It was official policy to believe the world stopped once it could no longer be seen.

The thing was, after Eddie disappeared, nothing was quite the same. The long days waiting for garbage became long days filled with dread and guilt. Four children didn't seem enough—there always seemed now to be an absent fifth, a silent whining presence that wasn't quite there.

One afternoon, not long after Eddie was given and then taken away, Mimi and Natasha sat together on the hill above the hut. Natasha put her head in Mimi's lap and wriggled from side to side. Mimi, out of habit, ran her fingers through the toddler's curls. The kid would probably fall asleep right there. She did it fairly often, sometimes twice a week—or was it twice a day? When it happened, Mimi was stuck, afraid to move now that the baby had finally fallen asleep. She wished just once Natasha would collapse on Luisa's lap. But she never did. The youngest found the oldest, always, as if by instinct. Natasha tugged at her skirt, and reluctantly Mimi started telling a story.

"There have always been children on this island," she said.

Natasha hummed and sucked her thumb.

"The world wouldn't know what to do without us. The world should be holding its breath hoping we don't find our way out of this place. It should be praying that we never grow up, that we just stay here forever cleaning up its trash. The world should be sending us giant fruit baskets to say thank you. But nobody likes to think about it. So instead of saying thank you, the world pretends we don't exist. And sends us its trash. And ignores the first law of thermodynamics—energy within a closed system is constant. It can be transformed, but it never goes away." Mimi had been glancing through a physics textbook recently. It was hard to throw away books without at least taking a peek inside. She'd read a little before heaving it over the fence. "What is the world if it isn't a closed system? Pretend for a minute that garbage is the same thing as energy. The world puts its crap out in a bucket on the street for Monday's pickup and it says that's the same thing as making it disappear. But it never disappears. All that crap ends up on this island, and we're nothing more than universal garbage collectors. In a way, you could think of the pigs as transformed garbage. They get bigger and bigger and bigger, but they can't go away. Imagine what would happen if they did."

Natasha rubbed her cheek against Mimi's thigh and drooled just a little bit.

Luisa walked up the hill and collapsed in the grass beside them. She'd been depressed ever since they woke up in the net with Eddie gone. And she wasn't the kind of person to talk about being depressed. Instead she kicked things, and muttered under her breath about building a boat, and pushed other people away. Look at her now—close by, but with her back turned to them like she didn't want to be there. Mimi knew she blamed herself. They'd shifted Eddie toward the edge of the net, sure. But what were they supposed to do? Wait around for the grown-ups to come at them with knives?

She continued with her story.

"One day, a boy arrived on the island and at first the children misunderstood. They thought the rules of the system had changed. They thought there was more the world wanted to send them than garbage. They tried to make him one of them. They showed him what to eat and where to sleep and what to do with all the trash that kept washing onto shore. They explained to him about how they were saving the world from being buried under its own vast mountains of discarded junk. They thought he'd understand the nobility of their purpose, but he didn't. He didn't even listen to them about the basic rules of when to keep away from the sea. Eventually they realized he was garbage just like everything else. Eventually the children realized that the world was doing exactly the right thing by throwing him away."

Luisa shaded her eyes. She picked up a stone and threw it at her bare foot. She picked up another stone and did the same thing again. Her foot would be speckled with bruises if she kept it up. Mimi couldn't tell whether she had been listening.

"The only mistake the children made was in thinking that if you look like a child, you also act like a child," she said. "The only mistake they made was in getting too interested in the garbage." Mimi lifted her hand off Natasha's head and patted Luisa's shoulder. Luisa didn't look at her, but she also didn't pull away. Mimi started humming a song. Natasha smiled and sighed and hummed a little, too, and then nestled in further.

Mimi had just reached the chorus when Natasha sat up with a start and clapped her chubby hand across Mimi's mouth.

"I hate it when he adds too much vermouth," they heard, then.

"You're right, he makes terrible drinks."

"You wouldn't believe the hangovers they give me. It's like someone's stomping on my head with steel-toed boots."

"Poor thing."

"I know. I certainly am a poor thing today."

The girls jumped off the rock and scrambled into the bushes.

"The new one will rub your head."

"Do you think so? I hope he will. He's got beautiful hands. So smooth."

They came along the path, two of them in high heels, smoking cigarettes out of long, black holders. Their perfume spread out ahead of them, sweet and complicated and unlike anything that came from the earth. One had red hair that looked as though it had been lacquered, and the other wore a hat with a veil. They had their arms linked, and walked with strong, confident steps. They looked almost innocent, like they'd be happy if they could spend all their days at a garden party. Mimi shook her head—there she was making that same mistake again. Innocence shouldn't ever be assumed. Who knew what they'd done to Eddie? They'd probably laughed and watched him bleed. Mimi tried hard to keep from thinking about it.

What did the grown-ups really want? And how many of them were there, anyway?

Luisa's theory was that there was an endless amount. She said that if she had the courage and the endurance, she'd kick them endlessly in the shins.

Andrew thought it didn't matter how many grown-ups there were, that the only thing that mattered was that they could do whatever they wanted.

Mimi's theory was that it was just six, but that they kept changing clothes—and privately, to herself, she thought she could look at each of their outfits forever. She loved their clothes. She loved the way they could put anything together and make it seem effortlessly stylish. She would die before she told anyone else that, though, before she told anyone that she'd love to see her reflection in a mirror, draped in a satin sheath, her shoulders hung with fur.

Natasha just batted her eyes and hummed whenever they tried to figure it out.

The two grown-ups stopped now in front of the bushes where the children hid.

"Do you smell them?" the veiled one said.

"Children?" The other said. She sniffed the air; then let out a mouthful of smoke.

"Even after a bath they smell like animals."

"They might as well *be* animals. The new one says they cry at night."

"Isn't that sweet!"

"I know. So sweet."

They started walking again. Their dresses were tight, but they had slits in the back and they took long steps. Their heels clacked on the stones. Their laughter and perfume trailed behind them even after they disappeared over a hill.

Mimi sniffed her armpits. Did she smell? She washed as best she could, but maybe they were right. She poked Natasha to see if she would make a sound. The kid surprised her all the time—how was it that her hearing was better than anyone else's? She wanted badly to know what Natasha's voice sounded like, to get an explanation, but the kid just shook her head and kept her lips pushed tight together.

Andrew sat cross-legged in the grass at the bottom of the hill and stared at the sleeping pigs. They lay with their legs splayed front and back, sacked out on the soft dirt under the shade of an olive tree. They murmured in their sleep, and shifted, sometimes, and murmured again. Their sides heaved as they dreamed. Andrew, staring at the pigs, thought he could see traces of a time before the island—not their time, but his. Sometimes, for even less than a moment, he thought their bristly skin grew clear. Beneath its surface everything that had ever disappeared inside them became visible again. Why shouldn't his life become visible as well?

The children didn't spend much time talking about the pigs, but when they did, they speculated about who might have put them there. Someone strong, they thought. Someone unafraid of sharp teeth. Someone who didn't mind the hard work of getting gigantic pigs onto an island in the middle of the ocean, and someone confident enough to leave them there to do their work. Once, the children had played at making an altar. They'd collected smooth-edged stones and piled them into a little tower in the hollow of a hill. They'd bowed down in front of the stones and touched their foreheads to the earth, and Mimi had chanted something in a monotone about thanking a god for building a fence between them and the pigs, but it had all seemed too serious and, even to them, a little pretentious. They'd knocked the tower down and thrown the stones at a target instead. Andrew had won that game, of course. He was more coordinated than any of the girls.

Looking at the pigs, he remembered being bounced on someone's shoulder. He remembered someone playing with his feet. He remembered someone stroking his hair at night while he curled up in bed, and the sound of cars outside, sirens, the whirring of a city. He liked to think about that while he watched the pigs. He liked to sing the pigs scraps of songs he remembered from those days. He liked to tell the pigs stories about the city. They chewed on them in their sleep.

"Once," he said, "my mother took me on the subway and the stroller nearly got caught in a closing door. A homeless man jumped up to help her, and she pulled me through. She was secretly relieved when the door slammed shut and he was left on the platform looking in.

"Once," he said, "we rode the ferry and a man in a suit gave her a silver dollar. 'Give it to him when he grows up,' he said. 'Tell him he'll save the world.' She kept the coin locked in a drawer. She said I was too young to keep it safe.

"Once," he said, "my mother and father had a fight. They were fighting about my mother being pregnant. They thought I was too young to understand. Neither of them wanted another child, but they couldn't agree on what to do. All they could do was blame each other. I wanted to tell them that whatever they decided would be all right with me. I wanted to tell them that I liked being alone, that I didn't need a sister or a brother. They thought I was crying for no reason, and it made them even angrier. It was awful. My mother ended up sleeping in bed next to me, crying all night, turning her back to me when I cried too.

"Once," he said, "I lived in a city. The buildings were so tall you'd think they reached the sky. It was unbelievable that anyone thought to build them that high. You'd think they were trying to climb all the way up to God."

Andrew could go on and on once he got started. The pigs listened to him with their eyes shut. They might have been asleep, but they smiled and sighed when he fell silent, as if they were patiently waiting for him to continue.

Up on the hill, Natasha collapsed again on Mimi's lap, and Mimi shook her head and whispered that she would never wear velvet on a day like this.

"That one with the red hair?" she said. "She should stick to silk. The velvet just makes her look fat."

Luisa was willing to talk now. She scrunched her eyes shut like she was trying to picture the grown-ups in front of her. She picked a blade of grass and chewed on it and then took it out of her mouth and said, "I like velvet better. It's weird to see it on such a hot day, but I think it goes a long way toward hiding the flaws in the female form."

"I disagree," Mimi said. Luisa was just repeating something that she'd said to her once. She tried to remember which magazine she'd read it in before she'd thrown it to the pigs. Mimi was the only one who really paid attention to what the grown-ups wore. She wished just once she could try on one of their outfits. Not even one of the really fancy ones, just something nicely tailored. Even just a pencil skirt.

"But velvet's so soft," Luisa said. "I touched it once. Old curtains. I once tossed velvet curtains to the pigs."

"You don't know anything about fashion," Mimi said. "Don't even try."

Luisa's face hardened, and she turned away. She picked up a rock and tossed it as far as she could. It didn't go that far, but it hit the tree she was aiming at. She looked surprised, and picked another rock up and threw it, too. This one missed.

Mimi never knew why sometimes she said the things she did, why occasionally words came out with no purpose other than to be mean, but she couldn't help herself. And anyway, it was true. Luisa was twelve years old and barely even knew how to braid her own hair. What had she been doing with her time? If Mimi had hair that could grow as long as Luisa's, she'd take care of it. She sniffed herself again. Maybe she did smell.

She pressed her finger into Natasha's cheek. The kid didn't move. She was asleep. Mimi turned and looked at Andrew, sitting below them on the grass beside the pen. Probably telling stories to the pigs again. Mimi had no interest in his stories. She was much more interested in the situation among the grown-ups. The new one? There was never anyone new on the island. But that wasn't right. Eddie had been new, and that was just days ago. Or maybe weeks. It was so hard to keep track of time. *Stop thinking about him*, she whispered to herself. *Just stop.* She thought instead about how the grown-ups came and went from the island. Maybe there was a dock somewhere, a private landing for a yacht, or a seaplane, or even a rowboat. Maybe there was a magic door in their villa that opened to Paris, or Rome, or Bombay. Maybe the rules were entirely different for the grown-ups. She said this out loud and Luisa, jarred out of her sulk, laughed: of course the rules were different. If there was anything they could be sure of, it was that the grown-ups' world was entirely different from their own. Maybe the island wasn't an island at all, and only the grown-ups could see land where the ocean was. Maybe the grown-ups could walk on water. Maybe the grown-ups turned into birds at night and flew away.

Natasha's breathing evened out and turned into a kind of purring sound, and she kneaded her thumb inside her fist like a kitten kneads its paws.

Mimi sighed. Her legs were cramping. She decided to risk it and pick up the sleeping child. Natasha's curly head collapsed against Mimi's shoulder. Her breath was wet on Mimi's skin, her whole body silky with sleep. Mimi carried her down to the hut, pried the door open with her foot, and laid her down on a mat. She pushed the curls off the kid's forehead and pulled a blanket up to her chin. Then she went back outside, and climbed back up the hill, and flopped down again next to Luisa. She could see that Luisa had been crying while she was gone, but she seemed to have gotten over it. Mimi poked her. Luisa shrugged and poked her back.

Mimi could hear Andrew humming, and she could see him sitting with his back to a tree. She saw a single cloud in the sky, drifting toward the sun in a lazy way. And she saw a ship edging its way along the horizon.

"I don't know how many grown-ups there are," Luisa said. "The most I ever count is five, maybe six, but the ones I count are always different. I'm not sure I've ever seen them all together. Sometimes it's hard for me to see things."

"When they had us in that net, I tried to count but it was hard to keep track of them. They all pretty much look the same. Or anyway they act the same. I don't know." Mimi was shading her eyes to watch the ship. It was far away, but even far away they could see that it was beaten up, a rusting cargo ship probably. It belched dark smoke that pointed to oil burning. "What do you think it's going to drop?" she said.

"Broken mirrors?" Luisa said. "DVDs? Old furniture? Could be anything."

"I wish sometimes they narrowed the possibilities," Mimi said. "I'd like to have a sense of what's ahead."

"It'll never happen," Luisa said. "There's too much stuff to throw away."

Down below, Andrew stood up from where he was sitting by the pigs. He stretched and walked to the hut. They watched him yawn as he ducked down to enter through the door. When he stepped inside, the island looked so perfect in his absence that they could easily imagine he had never existed at all.

What came, came in a net. It was pretty ordinary stuff, actually, if you can call a net glowing with nuclear waste ordinary. They tried to wake Andrew up, but once he fell asleep he stayed asleep for hours. It was always that way with him. Mimi and Luisa ended up hauling the entire load up onto the grass on their own. The bricks were made of blue glass and were heavy, and neither girl wanted to touch them. They wrapped their hands around the net's soggy cords and dragged the load across the ground instead of even trying to pick it up.

The glow faded on each brick as it emerged from the water. The lone cloud wandered across the sky like a sleep-walking sheep and then snapped suddenly across the sun. The pigs woke up. The girls felt suddenly nauseous and each hoisted a corner of the net onto her shoulder and together they pulled it up the path. They hated Andrew for taking a nap when they obviously could have used his help. "Isn't it interesting how he's always asleep when we need him most," Mimi murmured under her breath, and Luisa nodded.

Even with the sun behind a cloud and the whole earth in shadow, the island radiated heat. It was a dry place. It hardly ever rained there. The landscape was entirely Med-iterranean, rocky and scrubby and filled with flowers that miraculously grew out of unwatered soil and rock.

At the fence, there was the whole question of how to get the waste over it to the pigs. Would they have to touch it? Each girl turned away and vomited discreetly. Mimi reached up and pulled a small chunk of hair from her head. Should they throw each brick one by one, or should they hoist the entire net up and over? Luisa said one by one, and she loosened the net and shut her eyes and grabbed a brick but it was hot to the touch and she screamed and dropped it and it landed on her foot. The pigs were pushing more than eagerly against the fence. Mimi wrapped her hands in fabric and bent down low and placed them on either side of a brick, and lifted it by straightening her legs. She threw it high into the air. The spotted pig jumped. It opened its mouth and the brick disappeared. It was like a seal at the zoo, if Mimi had ever been to a zoo. She didn't think she had. But she knew what she was looking at. She grabbed another, and tossed it high as well. Now two pigs jumped together. They knocked heads mid air, but they kept their mouths open, and the one with the lopped off ear slurped the brick down whole.

There was a frenzy now among the pigs. The girls couldn't throw the bricks fast enough. The air was silvery with shattered glass, but the mass in the net seemed to stay the same size. A single brick leaving made no difference at all. The girls slung brick after glowing brick. Their arms were getting tired and their hands, missing fingers, were not as dexterous as they might have been. The pigs were practically screaming.

"We're going to have to lift them all," Mimi said.

"Should we try to wake up Andrew?" Luisa said. "I don't think we can do this alone." A chunk of her hair fell out, too.

Mimi looked over her shoulder. It seemed crazy that he could still be asleep, but where else would he be? Even Natasha should be awake by now. They were supposed to work together. That was how they were supposed to get through all this. Small body next to small body could add up to strength. It always had. What were they if they couldn't count on each other? Was it possible that Andrew and Natasha were awake inside and just too lazy to get up and help? She shook her head. You couldn't trust those smelly children, she thought, those lazy children—all they wanted to do was sleep. And then she caught herself. In her mind she sounded just like the grown-ups.

"We'll have to get underneath it," Luisa said. "We'll push it up, and then we'll tip it in."

They shoved the net as close to the fence as they dared, then started heaving the bricks from the bottom up toward the top of the posts. But every time they pushed one spot up, the mass turned liquid, and the bricks tumbled to the ground in the spot they'd left vacant. The pigs were panting and squealing and rushing back and forth. Mimi's shoulders ached and her hands throbbed and she could barely breathe from the fear of inhaling radiation deep inside her body. She pushed and pushed and pushed, and then she felt wood.

She was right up next to the fence. Her foot was pressed against the post. Her foot. No shoes. The lop-eared pig approached like lightning, teeth bared. She jumped back. She stood up straight; her feet scooted behind her, her body balanced by her head in the net. And that was the tipping point. The net fell, bricks cascading like blue water, over the fence, into the pen, right into the jaws of the frenzied pigs.

Later, sitting on the hill, picking shards of glass out of their hair, the girls tried not to think about how long some garbage lasted. Mimi held her foot in her hand and counted her five whole toes over and over.

"I was dreaming," Andrew said, climbing sleepily out of the hut. "I couldn't wake up."

"Couldn't, or didn't want to?" Mimi said.

"Couldn't," Andrew said. "It was the kind of dream where you're swimming, and you can't get to the surface of the water. Or where you're eating, but you can't get the fork to your mouth. I was trying to wake up, but I just couldn't do it."

It was dark, then. The sun had finally set beyond the water. The whole sky had glowed orange, and then pink, and then soft purple with the red sun at the center, an eye dropping below its lid. It was the same boring beautiful sunset that happened every night. Music drifted from the grown-ups' place. Dance music, with clarinets and an occasional trumpet. They could hear laughter. They could hear the whoops and cries of spinning on the dance floor. When the children lay down, they fell asleep to the sounds of a party. They dreamed that they were lying in bed upstairs in an old fashioned house while their parents had friends over below, and that, if they could just climb out of bed to sit on the stairs, they would be positioned to sneak their heads around the corner and see them, the grown-ups in all their glamour— dancing, laughing, drinking, flirting, beautiful in the living room. But the sheets were soft and the pillows softer, and even in their dreams, they couldn't rise to see what it was they most desired to see.

Luisa crept out of the hut in the middle of the night and wandered through the dark to the pen. She knew the path by feel. In the dark, she moved slowly enough that she didn't stumble over roots and stones. The moon was almost full, and the path and the ocean both shimmered under its silver light. The pigs were asleep. She couldn't see them, but she could hear their soft breathing somewhere beyond the reedy brush that filled the pen. Given their size, it was amazing how they sometimes emerged so suddenly from the tall grass, invisible one minute and looming over everything the next. One snorted in her sleep now, and another grumbled as if in answer. The rest of the island was silent except for the sound of the ocean. Back and forth. Crash and retreat. It was impossible to imagine the world without that constant sound.

She had a pair of glasses in her pocket. She curled her fingers around them and bit her lip. They'd slipped from a corner of the net that afternoon while she and Mimi were hauling nuclear waste, and she'd used her foot to scoot them to the side and gone back for them while the pigs were eating. She shouldn't have done it. Not after the disaster with Eddie. *Anything that comes ashore goes to the pigs immediately*, they'd decided when they woke in the net with her brother missing and severed rope in his place. *Anything that we keep gets taken away. Better to feed it to the pigs first than have it taken away by some other means. Better to surrender voluntarily.*

But the glasses. She knew she didn't see as well as the other kids, but she didn't know quite how bad it was until she went for a little walk with the glasses in her pocket. As soon as she was out of sight, she put them on. The world changed abruptly.

She'd always thought that leaves on trees formed a kind of web that moved like yards of fabric in the breeze. She'd thought birds were just gestures of movement, dark shapes in the sky and then gone. The world through the glasses wasn't that way at all. Everything had its own crisp outline. The trees weren't covered with a soft mass; they were covered with thousands of individual sharp-edged leaves that pressed against each other and shook when the breeze off the ocean hit them and turned upwards when it rained. She saw a bird sitting on the branch of a tree. She saw it tilt its head, spread its wings, fly up into the air, land on a different tree, and sit there without moving.

She felt like she was eating the world, staring at it through those glasses—tree bark with its mottled browns and grays, small rocks at the beach worn smooth and flat and just the right size to fit in the palm of her hand, the pan they used for cooking fish that was burned black on its bottom and rusted orange at its top. She felt like she could gobble up every object with her eyes. She hadn't realized she was so hungry. Why couldn't the world be clear like this forever? A kind of unformed anger at what she'd been missing surged into her throat, and as much as she tried to swallow, she couldn't get it to unstick.

It was obvious why the glasses had been thrown away. The left temple was missing and the lenses were scratched. But given what they could do, why would anyone ever give them up? It was hard to imagine a world where they weren't the most precious thing a person could own. She formed her left hand into a fist and banged it against her thigh. She loved the world through her new eyes. She wanted to see that world forever.

Once, watching the pigs walk toward her through the tall grass, her vision had blurred to such a degree that she'd thought she'd seen six tall women walking toward her instead of six giant pigs. The women were carrying spears and shields, and she thought they were coming to hunt her. She couldn't move. All she could do was stare. And empty her pockets. She'd been carrying some stones she'd found. One of them was pink and had a white line running through it. She cast the stones into the pen and whispered about how sorry she was that she'd kept anything for herself. "They're yours," she'd whispered. "I promise. I'll give everything to you." The women kept coming closer and closer, light flashing on their shields, but as soon as they got to the fence she'd scrunched her eyes. The pigs had been clearly pigs again, and she'd thrown everything she loved to them ever since.

Now, at the pigpen, she thought the night would be clear to everyone but her. She banged her left fist against her thigh again, just like she'd done that afternoon. She wanted to take that fist and bang it into something hard. She didn't think the pigs would even like eating lenses, and the glasses were so small, anyway; she didn't think the pigs would even notice them once they got them in their mouths. But rules are rules. She sighed. She hit her thigh. She knew where the glasses needed to go.

Still, she was slow about dropping them in. She dangled them over the fence. Sometimes Luisa called, "Here piggy, piggy," when she held out food, but not that night. She just held her hand out and shut her eyes. From a distance, her face looked old with anger and disappointment.

The spotted pig woke up and heaved herself to standing. She shambled over, sleepy but ready for a snack. The shipment of nuclear waste had been harder to finish than expected, and the pigs had stayed up late eating the last of it. Her sides bulged out, and she had a peculiar glow about her as she shuffled through the brush. The rest of the pigs kept sleeping. It was just about midnight, and the moon sent shadows through the leaves onto her back. On the island in the dry heat of day, shadows were what the pigs had to stay cool instead of mud. But shadows gave them something else, too. They gave them the beauty of dappled light, of its patterns through the leaves. Some people say that humans are the only beasts moved by beauty, but the pigs proved them wrong on a daily basis. The pigs never failed to stop to appreciate the lacework of light through leaves. They appreciated the perfection of a beehive. The smooth gold of honey moved them just as much as the sweetness of its flavor. The pigs admired beauty as much as any of us do.

Luisa wasn't looking when the pig jumped and bit her pointer finger off. Its teeth were so sharp that the bite didn't hurt. She turned, and saw the glasses gone, and felt a deep regret for the clarity of her vision before she realized that she'd lost something else. The pig lumbered away, settling back down among her sisters. Luisa stared at the new stump which was just now beginning to well with blood. Something was wrong, but she couldn't quite place what it was. Oh, blood. Oh, another finger. Was this enough to cover the loss she felt? She crammed her skirt around the stump and set off slowly back to the hut, the fuzziness of the world

revealed now as flaw, any hope for clarity ground up and
buried deep in the spotted pig's stomach.

Otis started the fire with the glass from his locket. He used the nail from the crate to pop the glass from its frame. The photos inside slid out and landed on the ground. He hung the chain back around his neck and felt the empty locket against his skin and held the freed glass up to the sun. The sun concentrated through it onto a leaf, and before long the leaf smoked and then burst into flame. He couldn't believe it worked: the glass, the warmth, the heat, the wisp of smoke, the finger of flame. Who said he couldn't work miracles? He was so amazed that it took him a second too long to bend his head down and start blowing, and he lost the flame and had to start all over. This time he blew gently, his cheek wedged in the sand, and the flame blazed stronger. He fed it with the tiniest sticks he could find—he had a whole pile of thin twigs next to his left knee—and then he added sticks as thick as his pinky, and then as thick as his pointer, and then as thick as his thumb. In a minute or two it was hard to believe he'd ever not had fire. What was life without fire? He couldn't believe he'd been alive before the fire, alone on the beach without a flame.

He could have watched that fire forever. The flames twisted like dancing girls. They shook their hips and jumped over coals and dipped down low, their hair streaming out like water. He could make fire. He was practically a god. He'd never let it die.

The flames formed shapes beyond the dancing girls. A soccer ball. A ring. A bird. The bird's chest was wide and its hips were narrow. When it stepped out of the fire it was the ash gray of coals gone cold. It turned to look at him, black eyes glittering. It cooed. His heart shifted sideways and the bird lifted its wings and circled up, over the sand, and away. He rubbed his eyes and took a sip of water.

Otis remembered watching birds with his son. They'd lived close to the ocean, and when his boy was just a toddler, he'd take him for walks so Alice could get work done around the house. They'd go out in all weather. If it was winter and the wind was blowing, he'd wrap extra blankets around the boy and wheel him out in the stroller. The boy would be nothing but eyes, glittering eyes surrounded by a pile of blankets, watching anything in the world that Otis pointed out as interesting. He'd take him on the same walk every time: through a couple of blocks lined with houses to a stone gate that opened to a park that overlooked the sea. He'd push the stroller through the gate and onto the cobblestoned path, and the world would turn to nothing but wind and salt air and birds. He'd crouch down next to the boy and point out gulls and cormorants and occasionally a pelican. When he shut his eyes now, the boy's eyes glowed in his memory as bright as the coals at the bottom of the fire.

He had to get home. There had to be a way to get home.

Otis's stomach growled and he looked out to sea, and he wondered if he'd missed a ship passing while he'd been watching the flames. Just like him to get so entranced by beauty that he'd forget the purpose for which it had been created. The locket was hot against his skin, its metal surface heated by the fire. He didn't notice when the pictures on the ground, picked up by a gust of wind, circled once and settled in the coals.

The girls blamed Andrew for everything—was it his fault that he sometimes fell asleep in the afternoon? Was it his fault that he'd been dreaming when they dragged the nuclear waste to the pigs? He'd tried to apologize, but as usual they wouldn't listen. They were in the hut right now, Mimi wrapping gauze around Luisa's missing finger, Luisa kicking the ground and muttering about how it was his fault the world was so messed up, not the world's fault at all. Neither of them would look at him. Not surprising. They made him the scapegoat every single time something went wrong. He thought Luisa might even blame him for Eddie. It was true. He could have been friendlier. But even though he was a boy and Eddie was a boy, that didn't mean Andrew had to like him. What was there to like about that kid? Anyway, he wasn't the only one who hadn't been friendly. They all could have made more of an effort.

It was the day that followed the nuclear waste, and Andrew could still see a soft glow across the sand. It would fade soon. He looked at his hands and almost felt guilty that he hadn't lost any of his own fingers yet. The girls probably blamed him for that, too. They'd probably say something like he didn't spend as much time feeding the pigs as they did and that was why he'd never lost a finger—that he just didn't place himself in a position of vulnerability in the same way that they did. Right. He climbed up on a rock. The wind pressed against his chest. A lone ship was halfway across the horizon. Had he seen it before? Were all the ships that crossed their line of vision the same?

Andrew brushed some dirt off his knees and stretched. He hopped down and walked to the water. He jumped from rock to rock between wide pools, crouching to find flat stones, standing up to hurl them out to sea. After a while, he stopped looking for stones and started simply wandering. Up one rock, down another, the sea to his right, the curve of the island up ahead. The girls had no idea what it was like for him, being the only boy. He hurled a stone out into the ocean. He kept on walking.

Past the children's hut, the island grew wilder. There were rocks by the water, but then a cliff stretched up beyond the rocks. In places the water came so close to the cliff that Andrew had to lean his left hand against its earthen wall for balance. In some places flowers burst out of the vertical surface. In other places dirt broke away beneath his fingers. He got his feet wet from time to time, and the blue water felt warmer, sometimes, than the air.

Just before a curve in the shoreline, he heard a rustling sound that seemed to come from the center of a burst of thorny flowers growing straight out of the cliff. He stopped and looked at it closely. The flowers were pink, and the nearer he got to them, the more their petals looked like leaves. The rustling sounded again, and, looking harder, he saw a small brown dove, wings folded tight against the thorns. It seemed to be stuck in a hollow—it didn't look like the thorns were pricking into it, but it also didn't look like there was any way out. Andrew couldn't tell if it even wanted out. The dove shut its eyes when he looked, and cowered backwards, as if by cowering it could make itself unseen.

"I'll help you," Andrew whispered. "Just stay still."

The bird puffed its feathers, so now it looked like a soft, gray ball. Andrew reached his hand in. The thorns were as long as the first knuckle of his thumb, and sharp. He unwound the trap twig by twig, almost as if he were unwinding a willow basket. He'd never woven a basket, or unwound one, either, but he found he liked the in and out, the following of one strand to its home. The bird ignored him and he worked to free her. His fingers were so nimble that he managed to avoid all the thorns but one.

When he'd cleared a passage to the bird, he reached his hands in. He'd never been in a church, but the space he'd created had a church-like feel. Soft light filtered through the tangles of vines, and the interior of the space was dark and mysterious, but also had a kind of glow. The roof of the space arched up to a peak. It was narrow, and the bird crouched in what would have been the nave, if a small hand-sized hollow cleared in a tangle of thorny flowers could have a nave.

"I'll help you," Andrew said again. The one thorn he hadn't managed to avoid was stuck firmly in his right wrist. He could see that a little blood was dripping from it, and he could feel the ache of the pierce down to his joints.

The dove flapped her wings as his hands got closer, and the only thing he could do, even though he hated himself for doing it, was pounce and hold her wings tight to her sides and yank her out.

"Don't be scared," he whispered. "I won't hurt you." He pulled her right to his chest. He felt her feathers, and the thorn in his wrist, and her heart beating against his sweaty skin. Then he turned his back to the hollow so she wouldn't scuttle back inside, and he put her down on the ground and let her go. She opened her eyes and blinked. The rest of her body stayed frozen.

"You can move," he said. "You can go anywhere you'd like. You're not stuck here like me."

She blinked again. Then she turned her back to him and waddled along the rocky path. Water pounded on the sea-facing side. Dirt crumbled off the cliff. The farther she moved away, the more her feathers took on the color of the wall. He'd just begun to think she'd vanished when she spread her wings and flew up to another thorny flowering burst, out of the dusty blur her movement created. She landed on its edge and then waddled her way inside. The new thorns looked just as vicious as the thorns he'd cleared away to let her out. The dove crouched inside, tucked her head under her wing, and pretended Andrew wasn't there. He could feel her willing him to move on, and he almost cried.

He stood up and dusted himself off. He went back to walking. To hell with the bird. He didn't even look back at her. He'd never have to see her again, and that was fine with him. He was so thirsty. Why hadn't he thought to bring water?

It was just a short walk now to the place where this cove ended and the next cove began. He marked it in his mind and said he'd turn back when he got there. The beaches formed two crescent moons and were separated by a jutting point of land with a boulder at its tip. Andrew clambered across the sand to that large rock. Its pitted sides made it perfect for climbing. He wedged his toes into its hollows and pulled himself up to its top.

From the boulder, Andrew could see the entire new cove stretching out in front of him. The water lapping at its shore was very, very clear. He was just about to heave himself up on top of the boulder when he saw something move far down the beach. Not a big motion, just a kind of shimmering in the late afternoon air.

Smoke. He saw smoke. As soon as he recognized what it was, the wind shifted and he could smell it. It reminded him of something—an apple orchard in the fall? Waking up inside a tent? A fire in the living room on a snowy morning with a room full of presents still unwrapped? He wasn't sure, but the smell reminded him of something just at the edges of what he knew.

A fire was burning on the beach, and beyond the fire stood what looked like a pile of driftwood, which, once stared at, became a messy lean-to. Was that a mat woven out of rushes? Was that rock supposed to resemble a table? It was a campsite—what else could it be? Andrew stared and stared, expecting it all to disappear, but the campsite stayed, and when he looked away and slowly turned his head back, it was still there.

He crouched behind that boulder, the wind off the sea pushing through him, watching the lean-to for signs of life.

He didn't see anything for a long time. Or it might have been a short time—time might have stopped, the way it often seemed to on the island. Sometimes on the island there were whole days that repeated themselves, sometimes whole weeks: the same old food, the same old garbage, the same old bickering between the kids. Right now the sun seemed to stay in the same position in the sky, so that would be evidence for a short time. But the boat on the horizon moved to the center point of what he could see, so that would be evidence for a long time. And then it moved past the center and off the far edge and disappeared. It was so hard to know anything without distinct points of reference. His legs began to cramp from sitting.

And then, just when he thought he'd have to scramble his way down to the water if he was going to find anything out, he saw a foot move. A large gray foot poking its way out into the sun. Andrew knew it must be attached to a leg, but from where he was, he could only see toes wriggling. And then, as soon as he'd become certain that it was a foot, the leg actually did follow, and then hands, with arms, and then a head. A man's head, covered with tangled gray hair and no hat to keep it from getting roasted by the sun.

The man pulled himself out of the hut, stood up, stretched his arms long beside him, and turned to face the sea. He stood facing straight out to the water, and then he lifted one of those arms still higher and waved desperately at nothing.

Andrew watched him and tried to figure out, given his height, how they could possibly shove him over the fence to the pigs.

O tis opened his locket and stared at its hollow center. What had he done with the pictures? He scrambled on the ground, looking for them for the fifty millionth time, but there was nothing. Just sand and shadows and twigs to feed the fire. How could he have let them slip away?

It was so lonely here. The sea murmured and grumbled and even screamed but he couldn't understand anything it said. He caught crabs and let them go and tried to laugh while they scrambled away but they didn't even look at him, their odd eyes pivoting around, searching for a hole to hide in. He caught them again and ripped their legs off and held them over the fire and sucked the meat out of their shells and shook his head, wondering how they'd ever seemed anything more than food.

Now that he thought about it, he'd been lonely his entire life. How was that possible? He'd had a wife. He remembered Alice's eyes looking into his in bed in the early morning when they'd forgotten to shut the curtains the night before and the dawn came spreading over them like a rose-colored blanket. He'd lain there as the dark turned to light and watched her waking up, the flutter of lashes, the unfocused gaze, the smile, that moment when the eyes first take in light. He'd smiled back. Her eyes were endless. He'd reached out for her. And then the baby cried.

He'd had a son.

How could he have been lonely with a wife and a child?

He reached out and grabbed another crab. It wriggled in his hand and then he broke it and it stopped.

There was a strange shadow at the edge of the beach, but he couldn't tell what it attached to. He looked back down and brushed a handful of sand out of the way, searching for the edge of a photo, torn paper, a color from something other than nature. Nothing. Just more sand under the sand he moved away. His whole body ached. His stomach growled. Crab legs weren't enough to keep him going. The shadow moved again, just at the outside edge of his vision. He shook his head. Shadows weren't worth pursuing. Find the pictures now—that's what he cared about. But there it was again. He turned his head quickly. Whatever had caused it was gone. It could have been anything. That dove hadn't stopped cooing, and the gulls set out for sea every so often, and who knew what other creatures lived on the island. There were probably some goats around. He should make a spear. The thought of a goat roasting over his tiny fire was pitiful, but it made his mouth water just the same. He was hungry. He was tired of scavenging. He wanted to go home.

The log against his back was rough. His skin was rough. His lips were peeling. His joints ached. His body didn't smell the way his body should.

He thought about the other women. He couldn't help it. It made him cringe to think about them, but they had been so beautiful. Why did he care so much about beauty? It was better than food, better even than water. But what was it? The first time he'd left Alice, it had been for a short weekend with a woman he'd met at the grocery store. Her hair was blonde and it fell straight down to her ankles so that when she walked across the room toward him, naked, it was like she was surrounded by a curtain of gold. Who wouldn't leave for that? The second time he'd left her, he'd gone to a cabin in the mountains for two weeks. The woman who'd brought him there had eyes so brown they looked like deer's eyes, and fingers so thin they looked like blades of grass. When she moved she looked like a willow tree. But sexy. A sexy tree. It made him laugh even now to think of her. What had he done?

Alice was beautiful, too, with her gray, endless eyes. Why wasn't a single woman's beauty enough? What was wrong with him? Why couldn't he stick with one choice and be happy?

There had been others. He could deal them all out in his memory like a deck of cards. But there was always Alice crying at the end. Or worse, Alice not caring anymore. She'd barely waved goodbye when he shipped out the last time.

He pulled his scabby knees to his chest. He brushed the sand off his shins. He dealt out his life and wished he'd made other choices or any choices at all and that the choices he'd made or hadn't made hadn't led to this deserted beach on this deserted island with a deserted life back home. He wished that his natural condition was not to lose things.

That shadow—there was definitely something there. He threw another stick on the fire and stood up. He shaded his eyes and looked in all directions. No ships on the horizon. No smoke from the interior of the island. No twine to make a raft. The dolphins he could see playing just at the edge of the horizon were definitely not thinking about him. His body ached and the dead crab in his hand was nothing but food and he thought he knew what it would be like to die. He stood up, his body creaking, and waved and waved at nothing.

When the grown-ups grabbed them, it happened so fast that they didn't have time to be surprised. Mimi was trying to distract Luisa from her aching finger, showing her what she'd look like if she cut her hair. Luisa was shrugging away, wishing she could be down on the beach skipping stones across the water instead of pretending to be interested in what her hair would look like short. Natasha was making kissing sounds at a line of ants. And then all three of them were being dragged across hard ground, their arms held by hands that felt like clamps.

"We need some work done," a man with black hair said. He had a white streak where his part should be and thick fingers covered in rings, and he was strong enough to pull Mimi with one hand and Natasha with the other. A redhead dragged Luisa right behind them. Luisa could see Mimi pulling hard to get away, and she also saw when the man used his knee to wallop her under the chin. Natasha whimpered. The man shook her until she stopped. Luisa squirmed and tried to kick the redhead's shins, but the fingers gripping her arm just dug in and held her even tighter and positioned her in such a way that her feet kicked air.

Of course it was just the three of them. Andrew had disappeared again that morning. Nothing was the same. Nothing would ever be the same. Why couldn't they go back in time? Andrew would have kicked the redhead, too, if he'd been there with her. Why did he have to disappear whenever they needed him?

The grown-ups dragged the girls all the way to the villa. By the time they got there, the girls' legs were scraped and bleeding. The villa was spacious and white and had a red tile roof and a wide stone patio, and the children had spent their lives trying to avoid it. But the hunt seemed to have changed the rules, and now the grown-ups seemed to have a different understanding of the kind of work that children might be good for. Feeding the pigs was one thing, but it seemed now that they were expected to be household help as well. A bucket of bleach stood in a corner. The paving stones on the patio were soaked through with red wine.

"They smell," a woman lounging in a chair said. Her blonde hair was piled high and her dress hung down to brush against the stones. "Make them do the work, and then make them go away." The redhead and the man tossed the children onto the stones and crossed their arms and stared until the girls pulled wet rags out of the bucket and started to scrub.

Hours passed. The girls crouched on their hands and knees. Luisa's knuckles grew raw. Her injured hand throbbed so hard she could hear it. Sweat ran into her eyes. Natasha whimpered. Mimi glared. Luisa wanted to get up and go for a walk. She wanted to toss a ball around. She wanted to move. She wanted to kick someone. She wanted to punch her hand into the stone. She wanted to stand up and save her shredded knees. Nothing was getting clean. The world smelled like bleach. They didn't have rubber gloves, and her skin stung, and her back ached, and her neck burned in the hot sun, and she hated Andrew. All of them did. Sneaking off without telling them. Typical. They'd get him if he ever came back. Something bad. Worse than the grown-ups. Something really bad.

Luisa's shoulders throbbed. Her finger started bleeding again. She snapped at Natasha, agreed with Mimi about Andrew, and wished the day would just be over. She wished everything would just end. She wished she had kept the glasses and could stand up and shade her eyes and see clearly where the path was that led to their hut and know for certain when they would be going back. She wobbled on her knees and upended the bucket of bleach and she cursed at herself. Clumsy. She couldn't do anything right. And now the bucket was empty and she was the one who had to go to the pump to fill it with water. She was the one who had to haul it, full, across the grass, heavy and slopping out and stinging her legs as she went. At least it meant she'd get to move.

At the pump, she crouched down and held her mouth beneath the stream of water. Then she ducked her whole head under, water streaming in her hair, water streaming down her neck. If she weren't so afraid of the ocean, she'd have been okay with a boat that wasn't entirely watertight. She was strong enough to bail, and she could steal this bleach bucket and use it to take care of leaks. But her legs still ached from when she'd pushed Eddie into the surf, and her scabs hadn't healed, and she had to be honest—the way that water had made her feel, heaving all around her, her heart heaving inside her, was worse than kneeling in bleach. She filled the bucket up again. She hauled it across the ground, and she only stumbled twice. Most of the water was still inside when she got back to work.

By late afternoon, the girls had migrated to a corner of the patio, their heads clustered together while their hands moved back and forth. They had just discovered that tears worked better than bleach when Luisa heard a voice.

"I really need new clothes."

At first she thought it was Andrew—it was male, but young, and there was something familiar about it that she couldn't quite place. She turned her head, but she couldn't see anything. The grown-ups were in the villa. Only their voices carried to the patio. Something was cooking inside, and it smelled delicious.

"It's that damned pink lemonade. Spill a glass a single time, and the next thing you know, it's all over every single outfit I own. This island drives me crazy."

It wasn't Andrew, but it was someone she knew. She felt her hand curl into a fist.

"You've got to be more careful"—that was a woman. Luisa could picture her inhaling smoke through her cigarette holder and blowing it out through her nose.

"I am careful. It's the island. It has it in for me. I still don't know what I'm doing here. You make me wave the fan and you make me carry drinks, and you don't give me anything in return. My arms are tired. You promised me a friend. Actually, I really don't care anymore. I'm sick of everything. All I want to do is watch other people work."

It was the way his voice rose when he said "tired," and the slight whine with which he ended his sentences. Luisa could see his face in front of her even with her eyes wide open. Her own face, if she'd had a mirror. Those same brown eyes.

"Don't whine," the woman said. "Wine is for drinking, not for crying."

"Ha, ha," he said.

"Exactly. This island is meant for laughter. Enjoy it. You'll never find another place as good as this."

Luisa put her hand on Mimi's wrist.

"What?" Mimi whispered.

"Are you listening?"

"No. Why?"

"Listen. Tell me who you think that is."

All three stopped scrubbing. The heat of the island closed around them like thick cotton. The buzzing of the bees was so loud it sounded like a chainsaw. Natasha's curly head nodded toward the bucket filled with bleach. She looked ready for a nap.

"Isn't there any way to get out of here?" the voice whined through the window.

Natasha jerked her head up, and the girls' eyes met, all three sets at once.

"Stop trying to get away. Learn to love it. We have everything we need and a little bit more besides."

"But there's the new menswear collection in Paris."

"It will end up here before you know it. Everything new arrives eventually."

"I don't want eventually. I want right now."

"We'll get you some new suits. We'll get you everything you want."

"You're so generous."

"You're so handsome."

"I love you."

"I love you, too."

The sound of kissing.

The girls gagged simultaneously. They stopped scrubbing and held their breath, waiting for more. "It's him," Luisa finally said. "Don't you think it's him?"

Mimi shook her head. "They grabbed him, sure," she said. "But there's no way they brought him back to the villa. They came with knives. We're lucky we're still alive."

"It can't be Eddie," Luisa agreed. "No way." Her hand throbbed, and she listened harder, hopeful and angry at the same time.

Natasha stood up. Her legs were chubby and her cheeks were soft, and she could barely see above the rim of the wrought iron patio table. She climbed onto a chair. The sun lit her curls like a halo. She stood on tiptoe, and used her hand to shade her eyes. Then she opened her mouth. The world froze.

"It's him," she said. Her voice was like a bell. It cut through the air with a pure, piercing tone.

The wind knotted itself around the balcony, the girls huddled together, and two shadows stretched across the tiles.

Andrew slid down from the boulder and crept as close as he could without being seen.

The man's feet were twisted. His ankles stuck out like doorknobs. His toenails were yellow and thick and curled over his toes. His hair was matted into locks which dangled down his back and knotted together along the way. He didn't look like any other grown-up on the island, but a grown-up was a grown-up, and Andrew couldn't be too sure. Still, he couldn't stop himself from taking one step too close.

The man whirled around, lunged at Andrew, and held on tight.

"Are you really here?" he said.

His fingers were strong. It felt as if he were testing Andrew for fat. He smelled.

"Don't," Andrew said.

"Are we alone?" The man sounded like he'd swallowed sand.

Andrew tried to pull away. The fingers held on. They were like claws, or like the teeth of a trap. Andrew thought about the bird he'd freed, about how the first thing she'd done was scoot back inside her room of thorns. The fingers hurt. Would it feel like this when any grown-up grabbed him?

"Are we alone?" the man asked again.

Andrew shook his head.

"Where is everyone? I need food. I need to go home. You've got to help me."

The man's smell—sweat and shit and something impossible to recognize—was almost unbearable. Andrew tried to pull away, but the man's grip was tight.

The fire looked pathetic from close up. It was flaming, but just barely, and it was smoking, but not enough to really see in the bright sun. The man looked so hungry that he could eat a horse, or anything that even slightly resembled a horse and suddenly Andrew got very scared. Who knew what a grown-up might eat? Maybe he really was testing him for fat. Andrew looked around, but he didn't see a knife.

"You'll help me?" The claws wouldn't let go.

"Please don't hurt me," Andrew said.

It was like the man didn't hear him. "You'll take me somewhere else? You'll take me to your home?"

Andrew's stomach dropped. "You don't want to come back with me," he said, finally. "Really. It's better over here. It's nice on this beach."

"No," the man said. "I need help. I was in the water for days. Maybe weeks. I've lost track of time. I've lost everyone I love."

It would have been easy for Andrew to roll his eyes at that. Everyone he loved. As if having someone to lose weren't a privilege in itself. And the thought of rolling his eyes made him slightly less afraid. But he wasn't the eye rolling sort. And he was too scared, anyway. He nodded and looked straight at the man. The grown-ups would never talk about loss. Maybe this man wasn't one of them after all.

The man let go of Andrew and started gathering up his things. Not that he had anything, but for some reason, he seemed to think he needed his hollowed rock, and a particular long stick, and he seemed to want to take his lean-to down and neatly stack the wood he'd used to make it. Andrew thought about darting away, but just as he was about to take off running, the man reached his hand out and grabbed onto Andrew's hand. "Can you help me find my pictures? They dropped in the sand when I started the fire, and I can't find them anywhere."

The man pushed his hair behind his ears. He wiped his nose with the back of his dirty hand. He tugged at his ragged shirt to straighten it out and then dropped to his knees and scrambled in the sand. The shirt was so worn it was practically see-through. His pants had huge gaping rips at the knees. Andrew dropped down beside him and combed through the sand with his fingers, not quite sure what he was looking for.

"You can't come back with me," Andrew said.

They ran their hands through sand. Nothing.

The man sighed, and looked at the fire, and pulled at the chain that hung around his neck, and then he stood up and kicked sand on the fire, and when even the smoke was gone he brushed an odd tear away and smiled and yanked Andrew up and said, "Let's go."

The shore was narrower going back than it had been on the approach. The tide must have pushed the water closer. The sun had finally shifted in the sky, and the island was quieter than usual. The cliff face radiated hours of stored heat. Andrew's own breath was as loud as anything he'd ever heard. His head buzzed. Sweat dripped into his eyes. The bottoms of his feet were thick, but still, the rocks seemed extra sharp now, and it was amazing how many steps made him wince.

The man's name was Otis. Like the elevator, he said in his sandy voice, but Andrew just looked at him and shook his head. There hadn't been any elevators to hit the shore of the island that he could remember, maybe because it's easier to repair them than to throw them away. The two walked single file, Andrew in front of Otis. It was odd that Otis wasn't panting. He was so silent behind Andrew that he might have disappeared. He carried his stick, and he carried his rock, but limping behind Andrew, only his shadow stretching out onto the wall beside them confirmed his presence. Andrew couldn't help turning around over and over, just to check that the man was still there.

The kid ran way too fast. By himself on the beach Otis had felt broken, but not quite this old. Now, hurrying after this skinny kid, hopping from stone to stone like he was a kid himself, he could barely keep up. You don't get much exercise on a ship. You don't get much exercise recovering on a beach.

How old was he? It seemed like he'd been away from home forever. His hair was so long he could sit on it, and so dirty it was impossible to see what color it was. He hadn't looked in a mirror in what felt like years. Could it be possible that it was gray?

His joints ached. Why wouldn't they when he'd spent who knew how long floating on the sea, and who knew how long sleeping on the sand in a crappy lean-to that didn't even keep the wind out? There was any number of reasons his body didn't feel good. He hoped wherever the kid was taking him had real food.

"Slow down," he called. The kid looked like a goat, bouncing from rock to rock across the water. Andrew. Not a terrible name, but not one he'd ever give a kid of his own. How old would his son be now? He could feel him nestling against his leg while they watched ships together on the pier, pressing into him to get away from the wind, or maybe just to feel his father beside him. His son, and he had no idea how old he'd be. He'd always been bad with time for as long as he could remember. He had no idea how long that was.

Andrew turned around at a particularly wide stretch and Otis gave him a little nudge to keep him moving. That face. Those eyes. Otis had always been a sucker for children's eyes. He remembered being trailed by a group of little kids when he was in high school. For some reason they looked up to him. They streamed out behind him, and it made him feel like the Pied Piper. He was embarrassed to even know who the Pied Piper was. The kids were like rats, but then two of them had taken hold of his hands and told him about some problems they were having with bullies. He'd gone back and shoved the bullies so hard their mothers had called his mother. Then some adult had explained to him like he wouldn't understand on his own what it means for a teenager to hit a little kid, even if that kid is hitting other little kids.

But the little kids he'd protected had said thank you.

Stupid story. Who knew how long ago that was. Otis shook his head. He was old now. He was living in the past. It was time to notice the world he was in. What place was this, that an eleven-year-old, maybe a twelve-year-old kid could wander along a beach, find a washed up old man, and lead him home without anyone coming and telling him not to talk to strangers? Otis pulled his aching self together and rushed to catch up with the child who was acting as his guide.

They were halfway back when they stopped for a rest. They leaned against the cliff where a misshapen apricot tree dangled a branch down from the flat land above. Otis stuffed his mouth with fruit and spat out pits in long, arcing loops. He wiped the juice off his chin with a crooked finger, then stuck the finger in his mouth. He grabbed the chain that wrapped around his neck and pressed its locket to his cheek. Andrew realized he hadn't asked Otis how he'd got there. A raft. Days in the water, maybe weeks. It was hard for Andrew to imagine. He shivered.

"How did you get here?" he said.

"I swam," Otis said.

"No, but from where?"

"From the ocean."

"I don't get it. Were you on a ship or something?"

Otis put another apricot inside his mouth. His cheeks bulged. His lips were slightly orange. Watching him eat made Andrew a little sick. All that chewing and swallowing reminded him that it wasn't unlikely that the pigs would probably chew and swallow Otis himself once he got close enough for them to reach. Or that it would be Andrew's job to push Otis into the pen.

"I was," Otis said. "And then I wasn't. There was a storm, I think. It's hard to remember. But the ocean held me up. It put me onto shore. It felt like lots and lots of little hands pushing me into place. That's what I remember. A feeling of coming home."

"This isn't your home," Andrew said.

Otis picked another apricot and turned it in his hand. Its orange skin blushed pink. He shrugged and tried to pass the apricot to Andrew, but even though Andrew was a little hungry, he didn't want anything that had been touched by those gnarled claws. Otis gave Andrew a little shove, and then they kept on walking.

They mostly walked in silence. Otis was good at ignoring the pain his bare feet must have felt on the sharp rocks. Or maybe they were so callused they didn't feel anything. He used his arms like legs, crawling across the places where the land between the cliff and sea narrowed to a thin, precarious strip. He grabbed Andrew once when Andrew slipped, and said, "Careful" in his gruff voice. He panted and he smelled and he mumbled under his breath from time to time that he'd like a drink of water.

The sun, once it started moving, moved quickly. By the time they got to the beach below the hut, their shadows stretched out as tall as trees, and the light around them was purple and thick, and the sounds of evening, the crackling of nighttime insects, the whisper of the rising breeze, had settled in. Andrew saw the dove in the thorns for a moment, briefly, in his mind, and then he shook his head and focused on the hut in the purple light. His shadow was long now, but when dusk descended it would blend in with the falling dark. The birds would quiet soon. The sea murmured like a restless sleeper.

The pen looked empty. The pigs were somewhere in the tall grass, but in the dusky light it was impossible to see them and sometimes it really did seem like they disappeared. Andrew wondered for the first time where they went when they retreated into the undergrowth. Maybe there were other worlds they vanished into. The posts that bordered the pen were solid, but the slats between them looked rickety and worn. It was a wonder they managed to keep the pigs inside. It seemed only possible, just then, that if it worked, it worked because the pigs agreed to let it. What if they stopped agreeing? What if they broke through the fence and roamed free across the island?

Andrew shut his eyes. He knew he should lead Otis to the fence, tell him to lean in, use his strength to push him over. If any human being could be considered garbage, this man would be the one. They'd made a mistake with Eddie. But to feed the pigs a man? Even one with sharp fingers and a horrible smell—he couldn't do it alone.

Andrew told Otis to wait by the water while he found the girls. The hut was empty, though. It was tidy, sleeping mats and pajamas laid out side by side. Even the crumbs for mice were strewn out in a nice neat line, but the girls were gone. He couldn't think where they might be. They were all almost always back by now, tired, waiting impatiently for darkness to really fall so they wouldn't feel like babies, going to sleep before the sun went down. The hut felt like anything that had made it a home was gone. Where was the mess? Where was the dust? Couldn't they have left even a single crumb out of place?

When he stepped back outside and looked down to the water, Otis was gone. Andrew's heart rose in his chest and the sides of his hands began to ache, and he wanted to cry. Everyone was missing. The whole world was missing. He was all alone without anyone to think of him.

And then he heard the pigs.

It sounded as though they were singing. It sounded as though they each took a part and grunted in harmony. A sweet kind of song, like a lullaby. A little bit mournful. A little bit like the song you might wish your mother sang to you from the side of your bed when you were a small child and she wanted your dreams to be sweet. If anything, it made Andrew's desire to cry stronger. It made his hands ache so much that his whole body ached, from his toes to his heart, as though he would never stop aching again.

When he got to the pen, he saw the pigs were gathered together. Otis stood by a post, his hands held in the air as if he were a conductor, or a magician casting a spell. He moved his hands in a way that looked as though he was cupping and shaping the air, as though he was molding the world around him toward his liking. And the pigs ate it up. They crooned and sighed and sang together. They stared at him with a focus Andrew had only seen them use for food. Their singing sounded like the sounds of angels. Otis smiled at them, and they smiled back with their long snouts and sharp, curving teeth.

Andrew stood in the shadows, his own shadow growing longer by the second. He could push him—do what he was supposed to do and be done with it. One hard shove, and Otis would be over the fence and on the ground inside. The sun was rushing to drop below the sea. The breeze was soft. Andrew held his breath, and watched Otis reach out into the purple light. The spotted pig smiled up at him. The skinny one rubbed her snout against the post. Otis's fingers were spread wide. His hand was turned up toward the heavens as if he held a handful of the light, and his arm reached out long into the pen. He turned his hand over, threw the light down upon the pigs, and the pigs reached up, but not for his fingers, not for his arm, not to chew him up and swallow him. Andrew stared. They reached up to push their heads against Otis's hand, to have their ears scratched, to grunt happily and in harmony for the dusk-filled light he offered them.

From a distance, seen from above, the island was shaped like a kidney. It had a wide curved side and a long indented side, and two shorter, rounder ends. From sea level it looked like a perfectly shaped mountain, all of it rising at the same angle to a peak at its very center. There wasn't any control room anywhere, no master plan for a magic island that served as the world's dump. It just was, and people just knew about it if they thought about it at all, and ships just brought their stuff there as if by instinct. Plastic bottles because no one trusted tap water. Fur coats that were splashed with paint. Television screens that simply weren't flat enough. Weight lost in weight loss competitions. Mothers' wedding dresses that daughters had no interest in wearing. Toothpaste samples from the dentist. Love poems written by boyfriends long ago. The ships brought it and slipped it into the water when no one was watching, and once in the water it vanished completely. Spools of film that no one remembered how to process. Dolls with broken arms. Income tax information that went back more than seven years. Half-eaten cupcakes. Half-read novels. Shrunken sweaters. Chipped teacups. From the outside, with perspective, it all looked smoothed and beautiful: the island's perfect peak; the sun forever setting or forever rising and never stuck at a punishing noonday height. But on the island itself, where even the idea of perspective did not exist, everything arrived in its particularity. From the island, it was the ships that seemed a single entity. What was discarded was unique. Who discarded it was not.

While Andrew was leading his castaway back to what, on that island, amounted to civilization, the girls were still hard at work and Eddie loomed above them.

Luisa could immediately tell it was him, even though the angle made him look as though he'd stretched so tall he could be at least twenty, even though his hair was dyed blonde, and even though he looked so clean it was hard to imagine he'd ever emerged from a barrel covered in grime. Was he wearing a suit jacket with a pair of shorts? His hair glinted gold in the sun. He was alive. She almost smiled. But then she flushed and she could feel her hands on him, struggling to pull him away from the ocean, but shoving him into the water instead, the angry ocean, the gray water heaving. And then she remembered the way he'd cried after that, his legs covered in sores, and the way he wouldn't stop crying, and the way he'd moaned inside the cave. And she'd climbed over him in the net. She'd climbed over him and pushed him close to the opening. She'd been so scared. But even scared, she knew being scared wasn't an excuse.

It hadn't been as simple as sleeping through the night. Andrew's hand had been on her neck and Natasha's mouth had been by her knee and Mimi elbowed her over and over for just a little more room and she wasn't sure if she'd slept at all. None of them let Eddie touch them and he didn't try. He slept as hard as if he'd been in a bed. She'd watched him that night. The moon shining through the net cast lines across his face. His mouth turned down at its corners. His breathing was even. He mumbled sometimes in his dreams, but mostly he was quiet. She couldn't stop thinking about what he'd had. A mother. A father. A bedroom all his own. She turned her back to him and shut her eyes and told herself she didn't care, and when the grown-ups came she'd kept them shut. In the morning, she'd emerged through the hole they'd cut to snatch him out, gone straight to feed the pigs, and hadn't talked about it since. She didn't want to talk about it, ever. She'd let them take him. She hadn't done a thing to intervene.

But now he was here and he was staring down at them and he wasn't dead.

"Don't look at me," he said. "Did you see that one with brown hair looking at me?"

His hair was curly and a little longer now. His eyes had long, long lashes and where once she'd thought his eyes were solid brown, now she could see they flashed with flecks of green. She wondered if hers did, too. His lips were full and soft and his cheeks were round and he was chewing gum and he blew a bubble and popped it and peeled it off his mouth and crossed his arms and drummed his right hand fingers on his left elbow. She felt a kind of weight lift off. Maybe she hadn't messed this up as much as she'd thought she had. Maybe it had been okay to let them have him. She scrubbed the tiles and her heart felt oddly light.

"I said, don't look at me."

The woman standing next to him shook her head and took a long pull on her cigarette. Her blonde hair fell down her back, loose to her waist. Her eyes were so green they looked like poison. "She thinks she's something special," the woman said. "Like she deserves some kind of special thanks for her hard work." When she exhaled, the smoke made Luisa's eyes water.

She kept her eyes down now, but she could see Eddie's legs. They barely had any hair on them. The sandals he was wearing wrapped leather straps all the way up to his knees. The straps crossed and crossed and crossed, and beneath the crossing straps, she could see red sores healed over. He had scars, but she had to look closely to see them.

"That work keeps you alive," Eddie said. He reached his hand out and took the cigarette from between the woman's fingers. He brought it to his mouth, sucked in, and then blew out. He looked sophisticated until he coughed. Luisa looked closer and saw that there were more scars on his legs than she would have thought possible.

"Darling, are you okay?"

"I'm fine," Eddie said. He handed the cigarette back to the woman. "It's just this air. I must be getting a cold."

"Poor dear. Your constitution."

"I'm just not as strong as I used to be. Sacrifice will do that to you." He looked hard at Luisa. She shivered. His eyes were cold.

"You're safe now. You're our boy. You know we love you. We would never put you in harm's way." The woman snaked a white arm out and wrapped it around Eddie's shoulders. He leaned into her, staring at Luisa the whole time.

They'd sacrificed him and he'd survived. There must be gods on the island, gods who actually listened to whispered prayers. She almost smiled again, despite her aching knees, despite her throbbing hand. He was safe. But then she turned her head to look up at him again. He didn't look anything like the kid they'd said was her brother. His eyes weren't scared anymore. She couldn't picture him inside a net, shaking.

"The brown-haired one won't stop staring," he said.

Luisa dropped her eyes. The way Eddie and the woman were looking at her, it was like they were looking at garbage, not like they were looking at another human being. She felt a sudden punch of dread. Eddie lifted up a sandaled foot and kicked it in her direction. She shrunk back. She wanted to go home.

"Look at her," the woman said. "She's wishing she could go home."

"I was not," Luisa muttered. She couldn't help it. She wasn't garbage.

"Did she say something? I thought I heard her say something." Eddie wrapped his left arm around the woman's waist. His right hand held something that looked a little bit like a scepter. He beat it against his thigh like a fan.

"She's like a little baby," the woman said. "She wants her mommy."

"I do not," Luisa said. Her voice was louder now. She could feel her face turn red. She pushed herself back on her knees, grabbed the bleach bucket close to her, and pressed its metal handle into her palms. "Stop talking about me. I'm right here."

"There it is again," Eddie said. "It might have been the wind, but I just don't know. I thought they weren't supposed to speak. Didn't you tell me they knew the rules? Doesn't she know not to talk to us?"

"I thought she did," the woman said. She dropped her cigarette on the tiles and ground it out beneath her shoe.

A wasp circled around their heads. Luisa breathed deeply. *Calm down*, she thought. *Calm down*. She started to crawl backwards.

"Look!" the woman said. "She thinks she can get away!"

Eddie laughed. It sounded like water, but not like the ocean. Like water in a kitchen sink, splashing over dishes. It had strange gaps, arbitrary falls while he paused to catch his breath. He turned the laughter off as abruptly as you turn a tap. "They're so cute when they're scared," he said.

If the thing in his hand was a scepter, it was a particularly long and thin one. It was maybe made of gold, or maybe of some less valuable metal, painted to look like gold but actually much harder. He held it with his fingers gripped toward the top, and it stretched at least the length of his arm below his hand. Above his hand, it formed a flattened ball. It glittered in the sunlight, and Luisa thought it might be crusted with diamonds. She noticed, too, that he had a crown of silver leaves twining through his hair. How could she not have noticed that before? And what was he wearing? Earlier she'd thought it was a suit, but now it looked like fabric draped around his body, a tailored drape, but all one piece. It wasn't silk—it didn't look smooth. But it looked expensive. And rare. His feet were netted in sandals, and his toenails were neatly trimmed, but they were filed to a point. He took a step forward, and crouched in front of her. The tip of the scepter rested on the ground. The light that reflected from it on the paving stones was golden. Now that they were at the same level, it looked as though the very light around him shook.

"Are you frightened?" he said softly.

His eyes were brown and flecked with green, and now she could see that around their edges they were rimmed in gold. His fingernails were gilded.

"No," she whispered.

"You should be," he said. "Do you want to know what happened after they cut me from the net? They put a leash around my neck. They dragged me across the island. They tied my hands with rope and the leash was so tight I could hardly breathe, and even the brambles that lined the path they dragged me up reached out to gouge my legs. There were two of them, and they took turns pulling. It was so hot I thought I'd die if I didn't get something to drink. I thought I would die anyway.

"It took forever to reach the villa. They told me I was lucky I wasn't dead. They told me I was lucky that it's never out of style to take advantage of small children. 'You're just the right height to wave a palm frond fan,' they said. 'We've been thinking we needed a houseboy,' they said. 'Someone more refined than a garbage collector.' They told me I had promise. And look at me now. Look how far I've come. Do you still remember who I am?"

The stones pressed into Luisa's knees, and she was grateful for the somewhat fortifying smell of bleach. She thought she'd never known who he was. A boy in a barrel. A shipment of trash. Someone to take the space between her and the opening of the net. Her brother. Looking into his eyes was like looking into the sun.

"They came with knives," he said softly. "You changed places with me. I know you did—you climbed over me in the dark. I could be you. You could be me. We were supposed to be brother and sister. We were supposed to stick together."

Were they twins? She'd never seen it in a mirror, but apparently they'd looked alike. Apparently they'd once been near perfect matches. There was no way they matched each other now. And what did it mean to be a sister or a brother anyway?

"I'm sorry," she whispered. "I didn't mean to. Let me go."

"Let you go? Go where? There's nowhere to go on this island. It's a closed system. I tried to run once. They had me waving a fan, up and down and up and down. They'd cleaned me up by then. Put me in a tub and scrubbed me so hard I thought my skin would come off, and clipped my nails, and dressed me in fancy clothes. My arms ached. It looks easy to wave a fan, but if you do it all day long it gets hard. I thought they were asleep, and I slipped out the door, but when I got to the top of the path I thought about you. About the way my own sister shoved me aside without a second thought. I decided I'd rather stay with the grown-ups. There's nowhere to go on this island. The trash comes here. We don't send it away."

"Please," she whispered. "I'm so sorry."

He reached a hand out. She wasn't sure if he was going to put it on her head or squeeze his fingers round her throat. Anything seemed possible. He had all his fingers. His scepter was as sharp as a sword. His fingernails were gold. Her own missing fingers throbbed.

"Please," she said again.

His lips curved in a smile. Even his teeth looked gold. Every single one was as perfect as if it had been shaped in a mold, poured and set, smoother than glass. His hand, the one with the scepter, was raised now. Her hand was on the ground, and she was certain about what came next. The scepter would fall, its point sharp enough to pierce her

skin, push through her hand and anchor it to the stones below. She'd be pinned in place forever—no need for a net to
hold her. His arm looked strong. The muscles flexed when
he raised it above his head. Everything around them, even
the stones, stood still. She gripped her fingers around the
bleach bucket handle and tensed, ready to toss it at him if he
dropped his hand. She wouldn't win, but she'd try.

And then—could it be?—she heard the woman's voice.

"Not yet, darling. Not yet. She hasn't finished the patio. If
you get it bloody now, she won't be around to clean it. You'll
learn. We have to wait for a new batch. They'll come eventually—they always do. There are children being thrown away
everywhere in this world. Once they've arrived we can have
a little more fun. Just be patient."

His arm was ready to drop. He shook his curls across his
eyes. He sat back upon his haunches. If he had glittered before, now his skin looked like poured bronze without a light
source to animate it. Cold and solid and heavy. The woman
stepped forward. Luisa could see her silk stockings and her
shoes. She reached an elegant hand down and put it on Eddie's arm. He stood up and moved backward with her. By
the time Luisa darted her eyes toward them, they were gone.

"Are you okay?" Mimi whispered. Her voice sounded
shaky, but the hand she put on Luisa's shoulder was firm.

Luisa nodded. "I was ready for him," she said. "I wasn't
scared. I was ready." She leaned her shoulder into Mimi's
hand. It was warm and dry despite the water it had been
ringing out of sponges all day long. Mimi lifted up her other hand and put it on top of Luisa's head. She stroked the
matted hair down smooth. Natasha scooted up next to
them and brushed her soft toddler's cheek against Luisa's
arm. Was it true that she'd spoken words less than an hour

before? She was silent now, and her breath smelled like milk. Together the three girls resumed their task. They cleaned stones until well into the evening, and even then they didn't get them as clean as they would have liked.

At the end of the day when the girls stumbled home, they found Andrew sitting outside the hut with a man named Otis. He was dirty and he smelled and his hair was matted and he mumbled under his breath. The girls nodded and walked over to a tree and sat down in the shade. Their knees burned. Their shoulders ached. Their skin smelled like bleach. It only took one glance to tell that the stranger was garbage. Andrew could feed him to the pigs without their help. They were done working for the day. Natasha put her head on Mimi's lap, and Mimi, without thinking, ran the four fingers of her right hand through Natasha's curls and bent down and whispered something in her ear.

Luisa closed her eyes. In her mind, she could see Eddie staring at her. She shook her head to try to shake him away. The wind coming in from the sea cooled the sweaty crooks of her arms. The pigs, grumbling in their sleep, sounded like doves cooing. The scent of roasted meat drifted down from the grown-ups' kitchen. She snorted. Like they had a kitchen. Like they ever needed to cook. At any rate, the smell was drifting down from somewhere. In her mind, Eddie stared at her again, his eyes hard. She opened her eyes and the world was exactly the same as when she'd closed them, slightly blurry, always just on the edge of focus. If she scrunched her eyes tight she could see more detail, and she scrunched them now and looked at Otis.

His knees were knobby and his skin in general looked cracked, and he was tall but hunched his shoulders in, and his face was gray beneath the sunburn. He reminded her of driftwood. He looked like he'd be almost as good as the pigs at eating.

"Andrew," she said. "Come here."

Both Andrew and Otis turned toward her. Andrew's mouth was open. He wasn't used to her raising her voice—Mimi, sure, but not Luisa. Otis looked like nothing ever surprised him, and all he did was glance up for a second and then turn back to the stick he was whittling.

"Get over here," she said. "I need to talk to you."

He came over, but the first thing he said was, "Don't boss me around."

"Shut up," she said.

"Whatever," he said. "What do you want?"

"He's garbage," she said. "Feed him to the pigs. And by the way, do you know Eddie's still alive?"

Andrew shook his head, his mouth still open.

"He tried to hurt me," she said. "He had some kind of scepter and he was going to nail my hand to the ground with it. He was going to bash my head in. Ask Mimi. Ask Natasha. They both saw it."

Mimi nodded. Natasha had her eyes shut. She squirmed her head around as if to say, "Don't stop."

"He was kissing one of the grown-ups. It was horrible. We've got to find a way to get off this island." She waited for Andrew to say something, but he was silent for a long time. Then he shook his head.

"Otis needs our help," he said. "He's not meant for the pigs. He was in a shipwreck."

"Does he know how to build a boat?"

"I don't know. I don't think so. If he did, wouldn't he have built one already?"

Luisa looked at Otis again. A broken man. Good for nothing. He looked as clumsy as she was.

"Then he's no good to us. If he got washed up, he should go to the pigs," Luisa said. She didn't care how hard her voice sounded. "He should go over the fence. Just like Eddie should have gone over the fence. Right to the pigs. Right now."

"Shut up," Andrew said. He lowered his voice. "I'm serious. Don't say that again."

"What?" Luisa said. "Pigs?"

The pigs were still cooing, but the cooing had grown louder.

"Pigs, pigs, pigs?"

"Shut up." Andrew's voice was urgent.

The cooing mixed with something else now, and Luisa didn't need to look to know the dainty-hoofed one had lumbered to a standing position.

"If he's a grown-up, he'll hurt us," Luisa said.

"I don't think he will," Andrew said.

"What do you know," Luisa said. "You didn't see Eddie. We did. The man has got to go."

"You should have seen him with them." Andrew's face changed. It was all lit up as he talked now, like he was describing a vision. "I know he looks like garbage, but they didn't want to eat him. They let him pet their heads. Who says we have to feed them everything?" He reached down and picked up a stick and threw it. It sailed through the air, and when it landed with a thunk, Otis stood up and limped over and picked it up. He threw away his old stick, and began whittling the new one into who knows what. He hummed something soft.

"Who says he has to go?"

Luisa punched him in the arm. "No one has to say. It just is. What washes up from the ocean goes to the pigs, and if it doesn't go to the pigs, watch out. That's what I figured out today. It doesn't matter if it's your brother. What arrives is garbage, no matter what it is."

"At least come and talk to him," Andrew said. He rubbed his shoulder. "He's different. Give him a chance."

Luisa looked at Mimi. Mimi's eyes were closed now, too. She had a red welt on her shin from kneeling in bleach all day. It matched the ones on Luisa's knees. There was more than one way to be a twin. Mimi was chewing on her lower lip. Her light brown hair was stringy, and a strand of it was stuck to her chin. She was the oldest, they always listened to her, but now she was asleep. Or looked that way. Now she was chewing on herself, and she looked almost as young as Natasha.

"What do you think?" Luisa whispered, trying to wake her up. "Should we give him a chance?"

Mimi sighed, and kept on chewing. Natasha sighed and scratched her cheek. The ocean sighed, and its sighs rippled out as far as the water stretched, the water exhaling into nothingness. There was no source of wisdom, anywhere. There was no one to tell her what to do.

"Okay," Luisa said out loud. "I'll give him a chance, but he'd better be worth it."

Otis smelled, and he had some kind of rash on his arms, and his clothes hung off his skinny body, and his nails were disgusting, but they couldn't stop listening once he started to talk. It had to do with him being surprised by things in a way that the children hadn't seen in an adult, ever.

"Really?" he said. "Garbage washes up from the sea?"

"Yup. Everything the world throws away."

"And you feed it to them? All of it?"

"You name it, they'll eat it. As long as it's been thrown away."

"Would they eat my toenail clippings?"

"Yes."

"Would they eat my yard waste?"

"Yes."

"Would they eat my dreams? The ones I had as a young man that I let slide by the wayside? I didn't realize I was throwing them away, but intentionally or not, that's what I did."

"I don't know," Andrew said. "But it seems like they'll eat anything. Try it. Walk over, whisper your dreams to them. I bet they'll eat them right up. Slurp them down and ask for more."

And the amazing thing about Otis was that he did just that. It didn't seem to occur to him that he might be garbage, too. Luisa drummed a three-fingered hand on her thigh, watched him limp over to the pen, and thought this was the time to do it. Andrew might not act, but she could jump up, run over, and push Otis in without his even noticing. Her body ached to move. Her body ached all through itself, actually, and her knees still burned from the bleach and she decided to wait. He'd moved too far away from her to see clearly, anyway. A surprise attack wouldn't work if she had to feel around to find him.

When Otis got to the pen he bent over the fence and whispered in a voice so low it was impossible to hear what he said. But the pigs heard, and soon they were dancing on their hind legs, their snouts in the air, mouths open, swallowing each syllable he uttered, each dream.

"That's a relief," he said when he came back. "I knew I'd turned them into garbage, but the garbage was festering and now it's gone. And look how beautiful those pigs are."

They were. They had settled down now in the fading light, their eyes fluttering shut, their long lashes grazing their cheeks. They nestled into a mass together, snout upon snout, six curlicued tails dainty on their haunches.

Later, Otis told the children a story.

"This is the best I can do," he said. "I'm playing a little fast and loose with the facts, but the gist is right. Bear with me.

"I was lost at sea. I was on a ship bound for unknown lands."

"Can you help me build a ship?" Luisa said.

"Don't interrupt," Otis said. "Where was I? We were becalmed for weeks: our food running out, our water running dry. I was the navigator, but without any motion, there was nothing I could do. We knew where we were. We didn't know how to leave. The captain locked himself in his cabin with a barrel of water and a salted ham, and the rest of us starved on deck.

"The crew wanted to mutiny. There were grumblings, and then whispers, and bony fingers reaching out to grab elbows and pull us into corners to plot. Not to have revolted would have been crazy—we were starving; we were thirsty; we weren't going anywhere. I wasn't interested in violence, but they told me that if I didn't join the uprising, I'd be victim to it. It would touch me one way or another. Like it or not, we were revolting.

"That's a joke," he said, but the children didn't laugh. Luisa was trying to figure out if the story he was telling was true. How could he work on board a ship and not know anything about building one? Andrew didn't care if the story was true—he leaned forward, his mouth open, listening hard to every word. Mimi was tired. It would be time for bed soon. Natasha was already asleep.

"Night was the only time we didn't feel fevered. Or maybe it was the time when our fevers turned more obviously to chills instead of to heat. I remember the stars I saw from that ship. I'd never understood constellations before, but as my body heated up and my teeth started chattering, I began to see the lines connecting the points in the sky. I thought the hunter would reach out a boot and step on us, he seemed so real and so giant and so close. I thought we were being measured on scales made of stars. I didn't know what weighted the other side, but it seemed to me that we were heavy, that our side tipped, always, toward the water.

"One night, the very night we planned to break down the captain's door, a cloud swept in across the stars. It was a gray wisp at first, like a strand of carded wool across the pin cloth of the sky. It made me think about my mother, and for a second I was a boy again, watching greasy matted wool being combed out into soft locks. But another wisp followed the first, and soon there was enough wool for spinning. My mother could have woven an entire shroud from it. She could have woven it and pulled it out and woven it again. I may have been the only one who noticed. The rest of the crew was so intent on blood and ham that they had no time for staring at the stars. They noticed the wind, though. It reached a finger out and tickled all of us. Then it opened its mouth and breathed hot air straight into our faces. The water, which until then had been as smooth as steel, reformed itself into hills. The sky was black with all that wool covering the stars. We only knew the sea was roiling by the feel.

We held onto ropes and pitched back and forth with the ship, and when the captain opened his door and called us all to order, we were crying and praying to be saved.

"Where to start about the feel of the water? It was cold, of course, that goes without saying. But I didn't notice the cold at first. I noticed the plunge, the shock, the way my body rejected the water forcing itself up my nostrils and down my throat. My body told it no, and my arms flailed, and my head tipped up from my neck of its own accord. But everything was black. The water was as dark as the sky. At one moment I was close enough to the ship to touch it, and at the next I was below it, and at the next I think it was far away. My arms finally stopped flailing and I noticed that my jaw was clenched to keep my teeth from chattering, and that I was holding onto something, and the something was a square platform made of wood. I leaned my head against it. I think I still have splinters in my cheek. The sun woke me when it rose, and I drifted, and the sun set, and I drifted, and then here I was. On the shore of this island, building a shelter, still waiting for salvation."

The children were holding onto each other's hands. They'd never talked about what life would be like on the water. They'd only privately imagined days aboard a ship. It wasn't surprising that the sailors had considered an uprising, but that there was only one captain was another thing altogether.

"Do you think you could have broken down the door?" Luisa asked. She could feel Mimi flexing her fingers against her palm. Her own fingers were like a nutshell enclosing Mimi's hand.

"No problem," Otis said. "Like I was saying, I didn't really want to be part of the insurgency, but I have no doubt that it would have been successful. The thing was, and I never said this to any of the crew, what would it have helped? We'd have access to the water, and access to the meat, but once that was gone, would life be any better? I don't think so. We'd still be stuck on that ship. They weren't thinkers, though. They mostly just wanted to throw the captain overboard."

"I wouldn't mind throwing a captain overboard," Andrew said.

"Yes you would," Mimi said. "You can't kill anything. Not even a spider."

"Shut up," Andrew said.

"You shut up," Mimi said.

"Both of you be quiet," Luisa said, and for some reason they listened to her. Probably because she asked another question before they could get a word in. "Tell me about the raft," she said. "How long do you think it would have held up? Would you have been safe on it if you didn't know how to swim?"

"I don't know," Otis said. "It wasn't really a raft. It was just luck that it even floated."

"Were you worried about the water?" Luisa asked.

"I was alone in the middle of the ocean. I was worried about everything."

Luisa nodded. She was about to ask another question when Andrew interrupted her.

"What was it like before you were on the ship?" he asked. "What was it like when you were a boy?"

"A boy?" Otis said. "What makes you think I was ever a boy?"

"You were talking about your mother. About the wool. What was it like when you were growing up?"

"That's a hard question," Otis said. "I can't quite remember the growing up part. I can remember being a child, and I can remember being a sailor, but how I got from one place to the other is as dark as the sea was the night of the wreck. Or as dark as the sky. Whichever was darker, that's what it's like."

"Did your mother make you sandwiches?"

"I guess. Sandwiches, but never peanut butter and jelly. Too many kids with allergies."

"So you had friends?"

"Sure. I remember birthday parties. Streamers. Candles. Icing so sweet it hurt my teeth."

Andrew nodded. Luisa nodded, too. She had tossed the pigs candle stubs many times, their waxy bottoms smeared with hardened frosting that carried the marks of children's teeth. The pigs sucked them down like candy.

"Here's a story," Otis said. "One time, when I was turning nine or ten and my father was away, my mother baked me a birthday cake and told me to make a wish. I shut my eyes, and wished I could see him—just once. My father was always away, then. He was like me—he worked in the shipping business. I can't remember a birthday from my childhood that I celebrated with him around. I shut my eyes, but I've always been able to see inside my head. It's the way I imagine, I guess. Very visual. Like a movie playing out inside of me. Maybe that's why I like to draw. Anyway, I shut my eyes, and there he was, pacing back and forth, a golden robe across his shoulders, a wineskin in his hand. He was always a king in my imagination—never mind that kings don't really exist, at least not the way they do in children's minds. But I saw him. I wished and I saw him. That's my story."

"That's not really a story," Luisa said. "Let's get back to the raft. How was it held together?"

Andrew hit her. He was staring at Otis like Otis was his own father. He had edged his body close to the man's, so his elbow touched elbow and his knee touched knee. He looked like he wanted to lay his head down on Otis's forearm, like he wanted to lean his whole body against the man for support. Luisa turned away and spat. "I'm going down to the water," she said. "Anyone want to come?"

Natasha wanted to come. She rubbed her eyes and jumped right up and trotted along the path beside Luisa and crouched down next to her when they reached the shore.

The sea was calm. It whispered in a strange voice that was almost like singing, but without any tune. Natasha tossed pebbles into the water, and for once Luisa didn't have the heart to yell at her to stop. The sea was in a mood, but the mood was gentle, and it was difficult to believe that it could ever turn around and harm them. Luisa's legs itched from the bleach, and her knees were sore from kneeling on stone, and her hand, her poor hand throbbed. The sea whispered for her to dip her toes in. It whispered that it would heal her legs and wipe away the memory of the day, the memory of Eddie, even the memory of offering him up in the net to save herself. But she knew better—she knew to listen to its song but not to trust a thing it said.

They stayed down by the water while the sun set. They were still down by the water when the moon came out. On that island, when there were no clouds, the stars were always bright. It didn't matter if the moon was full and hogging half the sky. The stars formed a tight path over the crown of night, and Luisa easily dreamed of walking that path into heaven. When they finally stepped away from the water and headed back up to the hut, Natasha was clutching a starfish in her hand. Inside, she curled up on her mat, the starfish pressed to her cheek, and Luisa curled up next to her. She listened to the sleepy sighs that filled the room. She heard

Otis's snoring, the heavy snoring of an adult so different from the delicate snoring of children. She heard the pigs sigh outside, and faint trails of music drifting from the villa, and, bordering it all like a ribbon around the hem of a dress, she heard the gentle sea.

Otis got up early the next morning and made breakfast. There weren't a lot of cooking supplies, but compared to what he'd been working with on the beach, what he had to work with outside the children's hut was practically a gourmet kitchen. The kids had a cast iron pan. They had a flat piece of wood to use as a cutting board. They had the pocketknife he'd carved up sticks with the night before.

He caught two fish—small ones that looked like bream—cleaned them, and tossed their waste to the pigs. Then he put them in the heated pan, chopped herbs, and even he, the cook, couldn't believe how fantastic the whole thing smelled. While he was cooking, he laughed about the bullshit story he'd told them around the campfire. A wooden ship. An insurrection. It was fun to see them listen, though. Their little faces and their giant eyes. And he'd told them it wasn't true. Right from the beginning he'd told them the story wasn't about facts. Maybe he could turn into a storyteller instead of a straight out liar.

The children crawled out of their hut one by one, their hair matted in strange patterns, rubbing their eyes, the scent of the fish drawing them out of sleep. Even the oldest one, Mimi, was cute in the morning, though she was a little too deep into her teenage years to be cute once she washed her face. What was she—fifteen? Sixteen? Too bad her hair was so stringy. He wanted to pull Natasha, the littlest one with the crazy curly hair, onto his lap and snuggle with her while she ate her breakfast, and he didn't even like hugging little kids. Well, except for his son. The best thing in the world was to hug his son. But other kids—he'd never been able to understand the appeal of anyone else's kids.

They ate the fish with their fingers. He looked away when they did that. Hadn't anyone taught them manners? But then he realized he was eating with his fingers, too, and their hands were a lot cleaner than his. He needed nail clippers. He'd never seen nails as long as he had right now. And on his own hands. They looked like claws, and they hurt his hands when he curled them into fists.

"This is good," Andrew said as he held his plate out for more fish. "Thank you."

"You're welcome," Otis said, and had to turn away. He was glad he had the beard and that his long hair hung over his face. Behind that curtain he was blushing.

Natasha patted his arm and blinked her eyes. He nodded back at her.

Mimi didn't say anything, but she held out her plate for a second helping, too.

Only Luisa, the one with the long brown hair, kept her distance. She took her plate and sat on a rock slightly outside their circle, and looked at the ocean instead of at the rest of them. He tried to make friends with her. He stood up to fill a cup with water and in doing so walked by her. "Is everything all right?" he asked in a low voice, thinking that if he were a kid he'd appreciate the extra attention. She just turned away from him and squinted at the sea. She had some kind of dirty gauze wrapped around her left hand, and she cradled that hand against her chest. Her nightgown shifted and he saw red welts across her knees. "How did you get those?" he said. She turned again, and pulled the fabric down. She put a piece of fish in her mouth and chewed slowly. He noticed her arms had welts on them as well.

Back at the fire, Andrew was scooping a third helping onto his plate. Otis sat down next to him, and Andrew scooted just a little closer so that his elbow was touching Otis's. That kid was so hungry for a father you could smell it on his skin.

"What's the story with Luisa?" Otis said. His voice was low. Andrew looked at him, but kept chewing. "Why won't she look at me? Where did the welts come from?"

Andrew swallowed, took another bite, chewed slowly, then swallowed again. "Who knows," he said, finally. "Maybe Eddie."

Otis nodded. He had no idea what Andrew was talking about.

Andrew swallowed again. "They're still angry with me—all the girls are, but especially Luisa. It's not fair. It's not my fault I wasn't here when the grown-ups grabbed them. Am I supposed to wait around all day to see if they need me? Don't I get to have some kind of freedom, even if it's just the freedom to take a walk?"

"Grown-ups?" Otis said.

"They're horrible," Andrew said.

"Do you think they have a phone?"

"Who knows," Andrew said. "Who cares? Who would we call, anyway? Nobody cares about us."

Otis stood up and started gathering his things together. He could be heading back home that day if he could call his wife.

"Nobody cares," Andrew said again. Otis looked at him, small there on the bench. The kid was starting to sound like a whiner. And he obviously didn't understand the pressing need for a phone. God—what if there was a way to call home from this place? Maybe getting rescued was as easy as lifting up a phone and dialing.

Luisa was at the fire refilling her plate—it was amazing how much these kids ate, given how skinny all of them were. She heaped her plate with fish, and neither of them knew she was listening, but all of a sudden she turned around and punched Andrew in the face. Not that hard. More like a pop than a punch. But it came fast, and it came as a surprise.

"Quit whining," she said, and walked back to her rock.

"Hey now," Otis said. He wasn't really sure what he should do. He couldn't just let kids punch each other. "Hey now," he said again, and he was embarrassed at how ineffectual he sounded. Anyway, she was walking away again. "Do any of you know about a phone?" he said. She turned away as if she hadn't heard him.

"You weren't there," Mimi said to Andrew from her seat by the fire. "You were off sulking, and we got stuck doing all the work. As usual. You think bringing him back here is such a big deal? You think he's going to change anything for us? He tells good stories, and he makes a good breakfast, but he smells. And he snores. It was awful sleeping in there with him last night. Great work, Andrew. Great work."

From up on her rock, Luisa said loudly, "The pigs look hungry to me."

Otis felt his face go red.

He pretended to stretch. Alice had complained about his snoring, but somehow he hadn't ever thought that he'd snore without her in bed next to him. Crazy. And he smelled? Of course. How could he not smell? He'd been in the ocean for days and then on the beach for days and then here, and he hadn't once thought to clean himself. He looked at his hands again. His fingers were coated with fish oil now, and small bits of dirt were wedged underneath his nails. He could only imagine what was caught in his beard. He couldn't ask for help looking like this. Who would listen?

"I'm going to go wash up," he said. "Maybe take a swim."

"You can't," Andrew said.

"Really," Mimi said. "You can't go in the water."

He looked at them. All the kids were staring at him now. Even Luisa, sitting on the rock away from the fire by herself had her eyes screwed up and was staring straight at him. Natasha, close by, had huge, round eyes. Her hair was perfect corkscrews. He thought he could probably stretch one out and it would bounce back into exactly the same shape. He remembered when his son was her age. Maybe three? What a great age. But his son had been a talker. It had been amazing to hear the things he said. This kid didn't seem to have any words, and he wondered if part of the problem might be that she didn't have any adults paying attention to her. He and Alice had made a point of talking to their son as if he was just like they were, someone capable of a real conversation, from the time he was an infant. No baby talk, ever. They'd played with his toes, but they'd told him, using real words, how cute his toes were. Natasha probably had no one talking to her at all.

"I'm filthy," he said. "I'm going swimming."

"Don't trust the water," Luisa said. Her voice was quiet, but it carried. "You have no idea what it can do to you. Eddie's still got scars from it. One time Natasha walked in just up to her ankles, and when she came out she couldn't stop crying for days. There wasn't even any garbage in the water when she went in."

Otis looked out at the ocean. There wasn't any garbage now. Come to think of it, there hadn't been any garbage since he arrived. Maybe the garbage thing was all in the kids' imaginations. A lot of the things they said didn't make much sense. Grown-ups catching children in a net? Who knew what to believe? The water was bright blue and clear as far out as he could see. The pigs were sleeping in their pen. It was still morning, but the sun was hot on his shoulders. His skin was starting to itch.

"I'm going in," he said.

"Don't do it," Mimi said. She stood up and walked over to Natasha and put one hand on the toddler's head. "It's true. It might feel good at first, but it'll get you."

Andrew, closest to him, just nodded and tried to hold his hand.

The water was the blue of gemstones, a kind of sapphire and emerald mixed together, clear but colored at the same time. It was crazy to think this water was ever clogged with garbage. Right now the beach and the water beyond it looked like those pictures in magazines where you look at them and think that every problem in your life would vanish if you could just book a week at a beachfront resort and go swimming every day.

He peeled off his shirt. He heard the children mutter something, but he didn't care. He undid his belt and tugged his ragged pants down his legs and off his feet and stood naked, imagining the water before stepping into it. He shut his eyes. He felt the water close around him in his mind, cool, but not so cool that it took effort to keep going. He felt his arms stretch out, the resistance of the water just enough to make the substance of the world real. He kicked his feet off the sandy floor and put his head under water and opened his eyes, and he could see: he could see as if looking through cut glass, as if staring through smoke without the smoke hurting his eyes, as if finally granted vision of a world he'd always known existed but had never been given the grace to see.

He opened his eyes for real this time. He was still on the grass, still naked, his back to the groaning children. Hadn't they ever seen a naked man before? It wasn't like he was turning around. Everyone had an ass. So what if his was hairier than theirs? He refused to feel self-conscious about that sort of thing, even if he knew how inappropriate it was to be naked in front of kids he didn't know. It was practically inappropriate to be naked in front of his own son, and his son was his, and a boy. Three of these kids were girls. *But spend a couple days tossed on the open ocean,* he thought, *and you don't have to worry about appropriate or inappropriate anymore.*

He stepped forward. He walked away from the beach to where the coast lifted just a bit. The water was deeper here—he could see by the depth of the blue. He stood on a rock and opened his arms to the sun, and the wind picked up and wrapped itself around his body. He could hear the pigs sighing in their pen, and when he listened, he noticed that the children were silent now. He took a deep breath. He tensed his knees. And then he jumped, really flying for just a second before falling deep into the water.

It was exactly as he had imagined it. The resistance, the temperature, the quiet. The water even felt good on his eyes when he opened them underwater. He couldn't see in the way he'd imagined he'd be able to see, but that didn't matter. What mattered was the way the water closed around him, the way he could touch the world, the way the invisible air he moved through in the rest of his life was made visible as he swam. He turned somersaults. He swam down to the very bottom and ran his fingers over sand. He curled himself into a ball and held the bottoms of his feet and stayed that way for a little while, knees up to his chin. It was the best swimming of his life. He nearly laughed, thinking about the warnings he'd received, thinking about the children with their stern little faces willing him to stay on shore. Once he was rescued, he'd bring Alice back to this place so she could swim here, too.

"Come in!" he called to them. "You've got to come in. You have no idea how great it is."

He couldn't see them, so he swam out a little ways and headed down the coast back toward their camp.

"If you don't know how to swim, I'll take care of you," he called, treading water. "Just wade in and I'll come get you."

It was a little wavy out where he was now, and he swam in toward shallower water. He could see the children sitting on the grass, lined up side by side, staring out at him.

"I'm telling you, if you don't come in, you'll regret it," he called, but they said nothing. Were they holding each other's hands? Lined up like that, oldest to youngest, they looked like a set of nesting dolls. He remembered playing with a set when he was little, painted lady inside painted lady, each parting midway down her dress to hatch an identical smaller lady inside. The children still looked like they were frightened, but they were far away and he couldn't quite tell what their expressions said. He felt something nudge against his foot and looked down. A plastic fork. He shuddered and kicked it toward the shore.

He swam what he thought of as laps, using two rocks on the shore to mark the boundaries of his route. He'd taken his son for lessons from the time the kid was barely more than a baby. He remembered watching him toddle across the tiles in a swim diaper and goggles, towel draped around his neck. He remembered climbing down the ladder into the chest-high water at the YMCA, the water just a little too cold, lining up with a bunch of other parents, mostly mothers, and then holding his arms out for his son to step into from the humid edge. He remembered all the other kids giggling and eagerly reaching for the water, and his own son too scared to even get close enough to take his father's hands. That's what those kids on the shore were like. They were like his son at swim lessons, too scared to believe there was actually freedom in taking your feet off the ground.

Something else hit his leg. A Barbie doll with her left arm missing. He grabbed her and flung her by her legs. The doll soared above the water, blonde hair streaming, and landed close to shore. His hand stung a bit when he put it back in the water. There must have been something on the hard plastic body. The sting spread to his leg where she'd nudged against him in the first place. He felt like throwing up.

He looked back at the shore. The children were no longer staring at him. They weren't sitting in a line anymore, and in fact, from the water, he could only see Andrew. He was sweeping around the campfire, tidying up after breakfast. Otis couldn't say for sure, but he had the feeling that Andrew wasn't looking at him on purpose, that he was concentrating a little too hard on sweeping, which is not a task that takes a great deal of concentration in the first place, particularly when you're basically just tidying up dirt. Otis treaded water and watched Andrew and wondered where the other kids had gone.

A wave hit him in the back of the head. He ducked underwater and when he surfaced his head was itching. Not just itching. It was like a nest of ants had colonized his scalp. And his beard. And between his toes. Another wave hit him.

For a few seconds he felt okay under the water, but when he surfaced again, the itching had turned to burning. The feeling that he needed to throw up had turned to actual retching in the water. He reached up to scratch his head and pulled a Monopoly game piece from out of the tangled mess.

He swam to shore with his fist closed around the little metal thimble. He could barely move his arms and legs—the most he could do was little flutter kicks because each time he tried to stretch out it was like a new set of forks started pricking him. The pain turned to something else by the time the water was shallow enough that he could touch the bottom. It was like each spot on his body was filled with the kind of pain that comes when you cry: an aching, throbbing kind of pain that leaves the surface of your skin and finds channels to your heart and then leaves your heart and pumps grief back out all the way to every edge you have.

He could see the landscape differently once he got close to shore. The girls were by the pigpen, sitting with their knees folded beneath their nightgowns. The pigs were at the fence, bodies pressed eagerly against its slats, small eyes turned toward the ocean. They were clearly waiting for something. He dragged himself out of the water. He knew the air was hot, but he felt cold there on the beach, his body covered in red welts, too weak to stand. He pulled himself as far away from the water as he could and shut his eyes and threw up and cried. He cried like he had as a kid when he was meant to come home by six but had spaced out and forgotten about the time. When he'd gotten to the door his mother had yelled at him, and he could see fear in her eyes. All he could think was that it was his fault, that he'd scared his mother, that he'd caused her pain and would never stop causing her pain, not once, not his whole life long. He couldn't stop crying. He would never see the world again except through a veil of tears. He cried like he had when his father died. He cried like he had when Alice told him to move out.

Who knew how long he lay on the beach. At one point, he felt a hand holding onto his gnarled fist. He opened his eyes. His vision was still blurry, but his sobs had turned to hiccups. Luisa crouched down next to him. He relaxed his hand in hers, wondering that she had come to hold it, wondering that she, in particular, was here to comfort him.

"Don't let go," he whispered. He could tell, even as he said the words, that his voice was too wrecked from tears to make coherent sounds.

She pulled him gently to his feet. He leaned on her. He didn't think he'd be able to stand on his own. She walked him up the beach, onto the grass. He stumbled and she caught him and he thanked her. At the fence, she untangled his arm from around her shoulders, took his hand, and spread his fingers out like the petals of a flower. The Monopoly thimble rested in its center. She lifted the game piece gently off his skin, folded his fingers back together, and let his hand drop down to his side. He shut his eyes, not wanting to see what came next, but he heard the pigs squeal in competition when she flung the thimble, spinning through the air, over their heads and into the tall grass behind them. And he kept his eyes shut when she nudged him, softly at first, and then harder until eventually she was shoving him up and over the fence, and eventually he and his aching, battered body were falling down, down, down into the pen.

From a distance, sometimes, the island looked like a fortress. Its shores were cliffs and its highest point was a tower.

From a distance, sometimes, the island looked like a whale. Its northern half was a tail. Its southern half was a head. The clouds above were the perfect umbrella of a spout. Passengers on ships passing by watched, breath held, waiting for the whale to breach.

From a distance, sometimes, the island was another ship. Flags were flown; whistles sounded; friendship was implied. Jokes were told about two ships passing in the night.

Always, from a distance, the island was far away. Always, it was just out of focus. Always, the viewing ship moved on just before the whale cleared water, just before a flag was waved in answer.

The children pretended they'd never met Otis. They pretended they hadn't tipped his wrecked body over the fence. They pretended that their hands were not the hands of murderers, and that they were only doing their jobs. Feed the pigs the garbage. That was their work in life. It wasn't their fault that the garbage this time was a wasted man. He might as well have thrown himself away.

They walked and walked down the coast, single file behind Andrew, who pretended he wasn't crying, until they reached the cove where Otis had washed ashore. His camp was still there. They spread out over it like ants, exploring what he'd left behind. The girls couldn't believe they'd never thought to venture down the coast this far. How much about the island remained a mystery to them? It looked wilder here than it did from the hut. The vegetation was thick and closed in on the sand, and the cove was studded on each side with giant boulders. It was easy to forget in that isolated place that the island held anyone else besides them.

They hopped from rock to rock along the fire ring Otis had dragged together. They ran just to the edge of the water and pressed their feet into the soft wet sand and ran away laughing when the ocean threw a wave in close to them. They used the sticks that had formed the lean-to as javelins, pitching them one after another across a line they scraped in the sand. They shrieked like ocean birds, the shrieks of joy.

Luisa spread her arms out and zoomed around the campsite like she was a giant gull. She was ready to fly out to sea, catch a fish, maybe circle back, maybe keep on going. Her arms flapped in wide, deep strokes.

Natasha huddled against a rock that had once been a bench and Mimi crouched on top of it and Natasha grabbed at her ankles like she was a little monster. Mimi giggled each time Natasha grabbed her, and she sounded like a little girl instead of like the moody teenager she found herself becoming more and more. She pulled herself up straight and turned into a sea captain and shouted instructions to her crew, and then the monster grabbed her again and she jumped off the rock, laughing.

Andrew tossed stick after stick, and the sticks were lances now and he was a knight. He rode horses and beheaded dragons, and went to the Holy Land on crusade.

From a distance all four children became a single laughing creature, all part of a tangled body that breathed in the salty air of the sea and the golden light of the sun and breathed out messy, chaotic laughter.

The pigs nosed him and prodded him with their hooves. Their rough tongues raked across his skin. He kept his eyes shut for a long time, waiting for pain and for the nothingness that might follow. Their snouts were surprisingly soft. The pigs snuffled and pushed him this way and that and then settled along the length of his body, heaving their enormous sides against him. They smelled like mud and sour milk and also like grass and wild onions. Their teeth stayed tucked inside their mouths. Instead, they licked his skin so hard that by the time he stood he felt like a newborn calf, wobbling on his legs, raw, clean for the first time in forever.

The children played until the golden light turned to pink and the sea inched forward to nibble on the sand and their stomachs told them it was time to eat. They dusted sand off their shins and their knees and their arms and shook out their hair and started home.

Halfway there, alone on the path, Otis waited for them. The sun cast its setting light around him so that his shadow loomed tall on the dusty cliff and his hands, stretching out toward them, made shadow creatures come alive. A dog. A rabbit. A flapping bat. The children gasped. They'd been murderers all day long and now they weren't. A miracle.

"I'm sorry I didn't listen to you," he said. "I'm feeling a little better now."

The children crowded close to one another and stared at him.

"Come home," Otis said. "You must be hungry. I'll make you dinner."

They shivered. Was he alive? Was he dead? He smelled like the island now instead of like something far on its way to rotting, but his sandpaper voice sounded exactly the same.

"I'll take care of you. I promise I'll take care of you," he said.

They looked at each other and then nodded and then followed him home along the rocky shore.

Dinner was fish again, and Otis picked grapes and roasted them in a pan. He plucked herbs from between rocks and made a salad with dandelion leaves and the sweetness of the roasted grapes popped against the bitter greens. He'd shoved the garbage that had washed up on shore while they were gone behind a rock and nobody paid much attention to the pigs' agitation. The children ate and sighed and leaned back on the grass after dinner and stared up at the sky and pretended they didn't know the garbage was there.

When the night got late, the children crawled one by one into bed. Only Otis stayed outside, splayed in a chair, his legs stretched across the stoop, listening to the pigs pace back and forth and back and forth all night long.

From a distance, living on an island is lots of children's dream. No parents. No bedtime. No need to grow up. Mermaids and pirates in the water, lost boys living underground. From a distance, living on an island is lots of parents' nightmare. Children turning into savages. Rival factions raiding one another's camps. Flies buzzing round the rotting heads of carcasses. From either distance the children ultimately leave. From either distance, the island gets tucked away as something to imagine but never to believe in.

Otis sat up in the middle of the night. The stars were bright and the moon was low in the sky. It was cold. He pulled his knees to his chest and tipped his chair against the wall. He could see the same patterns in the sky that he'd seen on board the ship: the hunter and the scales and the twins and the water bearer and the ram. He wondered if, once you've learned to pick them out, it was ever possible to see the sky as just a random mess of stars again. Sometimes he wished he could see the sky without it arranging itself so that he had to read it in any particular way.

The light the stars cast was silver. It cooled his eyes, and his body was cold, and he was reminded of winter and the way snow makes even a dark night light. He remembered walking from the car to the door at night in winter when he was a small boy, and looking up and wondering at the way the sky seemed to glow.

He could hear the children sleeping just beyond the open door, their breath soft and young. His own boy had slept on his chest as a baby. He'd traced his finger over the infant's lips. He'd buried his head in the infant's neck, the smell of his skin like the smell of life, spicy, indescribable, his son. It was as though a root were ripped from his chest when he thought of that boy.

He stared at the sky until he noticed his body growing stiff. It wasn't even winter, but the night cold settled deep inside him. He wasn't young anymore. He sometimes thought he'd never been young. At the same time he wasn't sure what it meant to be old.

He thought he'd changed somehow, but though his skin was scraped clean, a sadness lingered below. It was like every time he turned his mind over trying to find a place where he could comfortably rest his thoughts, he ended up in a memory he'd rather have forgotten. One time when he was ten he'd stolen an eraser from a kid at school. He hadn't even wanted it that badly. It was shaped like a cow, and he thought it was funny to flip it on its back and use its ears to erase the pencil marks on his page. He'd slipped it in his pocket and forgotten about it until the kid he'd stolen it from started crying. He'd carried it around in his pocket for weeks, too afraid to take it out in case anyone asked him where he got it. Every time he stuck his hand in his pocket guilt washed over him like a bucket of invisible paint. He wanted the pigs again; he wanted them to lick away his sins.

One time, well, really more like five or six times, he'd lied to his son—straight, look him in the eyes, swear you're telling the truth kinds of lies. One of them was about the reason they couldn't get a dog. He'd said he was allergic. He wasn't allergic to dogs. He'd had a dog in his twenties he'd loved so much that when she died he'd known he wouldn't be able to own a dog ever again in his entire life. But he'd lied to his son about it.

If truth be told, the children frightened him. He could have been hurt badly when Luisa pushed him into the pen. What kind of desperation made a child act like that? She had flinched yesterday when he put his hand on her back, like she thought he was going to hurt her. Like he'd ever hurt a child.

There was something else: just before he'd stumbled down the coast to find the children, he'd looked inside their hut. He hadn't seen it during the day, and he was amazed at how tidy these children were. All the mats were straightened and it looked as though the floor had been swept. But on the wall at the far end of the hut's single room, someone had scraped a picture with a charred stick—a boy with what looked like a knife held to his throat by a giant hand. He couldn't help but appreciate the artistry, but the image made him shudder. Who were these children? What did he know about their fears?

Those people living up there in the villa, they probably just didn't realize what the kids were going through. How could anyone stand by and watch children submit to terror?

He'd find out, he thought. There was a reason he'd been saved. Washed up from the ocean. He was proof that miracles existed. He knew his job now—it wasn't to get home. It was to talk to the people on the hill. He'd make them see the stress these kids were under. He'd save the kids, and he wouldn't go home until he'd taken care of them. The children needed saving and he was meant to do it. It wouldn't be hard, anyway. Sense made sense. Of course it did. He'd be home in no time.

He stood up creakily—really, he could hear his body creak—glanced inside to make sure the children were still sleeping, and walked toward the path. He looked up, but the constellations were unnecessary. On that island there was rarely a need for a guide. He touched the chain around his neck. The locket felt heavy and cold and he wished he could open it and look at Alice and his son frozen safe inside. Lost for the sake of a fire. Lost for the sake of living too much in the present. If he were being honest, they were lost a long time ago. He shut his eyes and pictured their faces quickly. He'd help the kids and after that he'd get home and he'd make everything better. He would. He promised himself he would. *Nothing is lost forever*, he thought. *There's always a second chance.*

From a distance, the island might have been mistaken for a funhouse at a carnival. Its polished rocks looked like mirrors. Its smooth hills looked like slides. Get closer, though, and the shrieks of laughter coming from its hidden passageways sounded more like shrieks of pain. Better to keep a distance and focus on the last time you ate kettle corn; better to remember that lovely mixture of sweet and salty as it melted against your tongue.

Otis followed the path through trees and around bends and ignored the unexpected ocean vistas that the wilderness occasionally opened to reveal. He was going to save the children. He was going to set things straight for them and then use a phone to call Alice. He'd be able to tell her he was safe. He'd be able to tell her that he, person-ally, had rescued four children from difficult conditions. He felt like how his dog of long ago must have felt when she ran to him, tail wagging, stick in her mouth, her entire body smiling. He was out of breath by the time he got to the end of the path.

The villa in the early light looked like something from a magazine. It was bright white—whiter than the cliffs he and Andrew had rushed by two days ago, but a little like those cliffs anyway, like those cliffs perfected. The pink flowers that twined above its blue doors were the same pink flowers that burst in tufts from the cliffs' crumbling walls. It all looked so still, and the air was so quiet—it was hard to believe that what he was looking at was real. He felt the first tug of hesitation when he realized that whoever he'd be asking for help from was probably still asleep.

But he was a castaway; his cause was good. The children's hut looked ten times worse now when he saw it compared to this place. Someone up here should be responsible for those kids. Someone up here should make sure they went to school.

He pulled his rags straight. He took a deep breath. He drew himself up as tall as he could and walked across the neatly mown lawn. The door was painted bluer than the sky. Come to think of it, the sky wasn't even blue quite yet. It was still a kind of purplish color. He wondered if he should wait until a more reasonable hour to knock.

But he couldn't wait. He'd been waiting his whole life. He'd been waiting forever, and it was time now to make a difference.

He stepped onto the flat stones that led to the door. He climbed a step and raised a fist and tapped on wood. The sound was so soft at first that even he could barely hear it, so he drew his hand back and formed the fist anew. He rapped loud this time, loud enough to wake a person deep in sleep. By the time the door opened, he was pounding, all the desperation of the days at sea, the days alone on the beach, the frightened, hungry children, his wife and child long gone, all that finding expression in his hand. He didn't even feel the bruises he was inflicting on himself. *Help me, help me, help me*, was all he heard as he hit that wood over and over.

The door opened inwards, and he almost fell into the arms of the woman who opened it.

If he had been in a state of mind to notice, he would have seen immediately that she wasn't happy.

Even if he'd noticed she wasn't happy, he wouldn't have been prepared for what came next.

"Ugh," she said. "Who are you?"

"I need help," Otis said.

"Clearly," the woman said.

He stepped closer to her. She drew back. He took another step, and now he was through the doorway. The stone floor was cold beneath his feet. He slipped and held his hand out to steady himself, and the woman shrieked.

"Get out," she said.

"I just need help," Otis said. "Do you have a phone I could use?"

"Stay outside," she said.

He looked at her, confused. Her blonde hair was piled high on her head. Her skin was so white he could see blue veins beneath it. She wore a long silk dressing gown, so long it trailed on the floor, and her slippers peeking out beneath its hem were trimmed with fur.

"You smell," she said.

He looked down. His torn shirt. His torn pants. His skin permanently stained, it seemed, with dirt that he just could not wash off. He nodded. He felt his face go red.

"What are you?" she said. She took another step back. "What are you doing here?"

"I just need a phone. Just a phone. I just need to tell my wife that I'm alive. She'll send help for me."

She took several more steps back. She turned her head. Her neck was very long. "Darlings," she called. "Darlings, I need you here right now."

"I'm here for help, and I'm here to help the children, but really, more than anything, I just want to go home." It was very hard to hold onto altruistic impulses when put to the test.

He heard feet climbing down steps. He heard doors opening and shutting deep inside the villa. He heard sleepy groans and gnashing teeth and the snap of boots on tile. The woman stared at him as though he were unlike anything she'd ever seen and as though that alone was cause for disgust, and when the space behind her filled up with sulky, angry faces, he didn't even try to fight. He just held his hands out and let them lead him away.

Otis was gone by the time the children woke up. The blanket he'd been using was neatly folded and put away. It looked like he'd swept the front stoop. He'd left the newest stick he'd been whittling on the arm of the chair, and he'd washed the dishes they'd used for dinner the night before. They ate breakfast. Without Otis it was just berries.

In the back, behind the hut, they found a note scratched in the dirt. "I'm a new man now," it said. "Off to make things better. Stay safe. Will return." They shrugged, not willing to admit how hurt they were that he'd left without saying goodbye and how certain they were that he'd never actually return, and how overwhelmed they were by the garbage they'd shoved aside the night before. They swept over the note with homemade brooms and pretended they'd never seen it.

Thank goodness the load of garbage that morning was light: broken Styrofoam coolers, empty plastic tape reels, bubble wrap. It weighed practically nothing, and the pigs crunched through it like popcorn. It was easy to drag the pieces from the night before over to the pen and pretend they'd only just arrived. The older garbage dripped, and smelled awful, and left the children smelling awful, too, but it disappeared and once it was gone it was like it had never existed at all. After they cleared the shore, Andrew cut some vines and braided them into a rope. They spent the rest of the morning playing jump rope games, two turning, two chasing, chanting rhymes, trying to remember the wildness they'd felt the day before. The pigs were interested in the movement, and they mimicked it beyond the fence. They could jump higher than the kids. If they'd been anywhere else in the world, they'd probably have been put into an exhibit: Amazing Dancing Pigs. Amazing Jumping Pigs. Amazing Garbage-Eating, Dancing, Jumping, Juggling, Sharp-Toothed Pigs. People would have paid to see them.

The children moved to the rhythm of the turning rope, and the pigs moved to the rhythm of the turning rope, and nobody talked about Otis's absence. It was fun, but there was a kind of tamped down quality to at least the children's motions. After a while they flopped down on the ground and just watched the pigs. It wasn't a bad morning. Just quiet.

But midway through the afternoon, there was a kind of commotion up among the grown-ups so loud it might as well have been broadcast over a PA system. Voices spoke with urgency: "My shoes need a polish," and "Who stole my hairbrush?" and "Do you think this looks good on me?"

And then a rough, strange voice said, "Let me go. You've got to let me out of here."

The children turned and looked at one another. "Otis," they said, the three who spoke; "Otis," they said as one.

"Did you hear?" The voice this time was female. "He says he doesn't want to be here. Would you rather be with the children? Would you rather be feeding pigs?"

"You're heartless," the voice they thought was Otis said. "All of you up here. You drink your drinks and play your music and wear your shoes, and you have no idea what you cost the world. No idea at all."

"You're so funny," they heard. "You're so, so funny."

"He's not funny at all," a sulky voice said.

"I was being sarcastic," another said.

"Well it wasn't clear," they heard. "If you're going to be sarcastic, at least be clear about it. I couldn't tell whether I was supposed to take you seriously or not. Hit him."

They heard a howl.

"Shut up," they heard. "Take it like a man."

The children stared at one another.

The howling increased in volume.

"I think we need to rescue him," Andrew said.

The girls stared at him and Mimi even rolled her eyes.

"Please stop," they heard.

Then they heard a scream.

Then all they could hear was laughter.

The children shifted so as to turn away from each other's eyes. Or, more accurately, the girls wouldn't look at Andrew. He paced back and forth, rubbing his hands together, worrying the rough skin on his knuckles, and each time he turned to one of them she nonchalantly looked away.

"Don't you care?" he said. Natasha sat down on the ground, picked up a couple of twigs, and set about turning them into a fairy house.

"Aren't you worried?" he said. Mimi yanked at her skirt, trying to stretch it so it would fall below her knees.

"I thought at least *you* would be willing to do something," he said. Luisa looked up at the sky. A bird flew across her line of vision, a blur of gray. It landed in an olive tree, and vanished inside the silvery leaves. She turned to stare at the ocean. The waves were an ordinary blue. A different bird flew across them and scooped water into its mouth. A pelican maybe. More probably a gull. It was hard to see clearly—bad eyes, why even try? She turned to stare at the pigs. They'd gone to sleep in the shade now like ordinary pigs.

Their pen looked like an ordinary pen. Her finger hurt. She shrugged.

"He's a human being," Andrew said. "He's not garbage. Even the pigs know that. He's a miracle. Don't we have a responsibility to help him? If we don't act, even when we're afraid, how can we call ourselves human?"

"That's not what makes us human," Luisa said.

"It's part of it," Andrew said.

"No," Luisa said. "It's just what makes us good."

Another howl carried across the air from the grown-ups' villa. It caught them at the back of their necks and skittered down their spines and settled in their guts. It made their feet itch to run to their cave. But what cave? Why hadn't they looked for a new one? Why had they been wasting their time?

The bird made another pass across the water. It dove down, and Luisa was sure when it rose again that something wriggled in its mouth. A fish, but what kind? She couldn't see the details.

"Please," Andrew said. He held his hands out to Luisa. She stared hard at the ground. "He needs us," Andrew said. "We have to get him back. I need him."

Luisa raised her eyes. Close up, everything was clear, detail after detail settling in place. She looked at Natasha, who'd wholly turned her mind to play. She was bending twigs this way and that, humming softly under her breath. She looked at Mimi, whose knees stuck out below her skirt no matter how hard she tugged the fabric down. She looked at Andrew, who stared at her like he didn't care if she saw him cry. She looked at her hands, the stump where her pinky was missing, the longer, barely healed stump of her pointer, the skin a deep brown from the sun. She nodded her head.

"Okay," she said. "I'll go with you. But I get to lead. And no promises. I don't like it up there, and I'm not staying any longer than I have to."

They heard another howl. They heard another peal of laughter. Then a howl. Then laughter. Then a howl. Then laughter again.

And then all was quiet.

Mimi lay on her mat pretending she was asleep while Andrew and Luisa plotted. Natasha was curled against her side, the girl's wet breath like damp fur on her skin. She rolled and stretched and caught odd words here and there. Enough to patch together their plan. Not enough to ask to be a part of it.

She hated being the oldest. Actually, she liked being the oldest, but it felt lonely. She had different interests than the others. They had no self awareness and she was all self awareness—she could never stop seeing herself from the outside. Her body wasn't even the body of a child anymore. She could tell by the feel of it that from a distance she'd probably look more like the grown-ups than the children. She wore a stretched out graying bra that had washed ashore one day, and she could swear the pigs looked at her reproachfully when she got close. She needed it. What was she supposed to do? She couldn't stay a child forever. She didn't want to stay a child—who does until they're an adult?

Sometimes her fingers hurt. The ones that were gone, not the ones that remained. She missed them. She'd never admit it to any of the kids, but sometimes at night she curled her hands into fists and held them to her lips and whispered to her missing fingers. Before the last finger had been clipped, she'd been teaching herself how to sew. She had visions of the dresses she'd make, long and clinging to her body—and in her visions her body was finished changing. Her legs were long and her hips curved but were still narrow and her breasts were exactly right for what she wanted to wear, slightly on the full side but not too full. The dresses changed color in her imagination. Sometimes they were red. Sometimes they were black. Sometimes they were the silver gray of the ocean just before a storm.

She was pretty good at sewing. She didn't use thread, or fabric, or anything like that—she didn't have them. She carved a needle from a twig, and threaded it with blades of grass. She poked holes through leaves, and stitched them into crowns. Everybody wanted one. Andrew looked like an elf. Luisa looked slightly older, and slightly more attractive, but pretty much the same, thick long hair and all. Natasha looked like a princess in her crown, a silent princess. God, when would she start talking? Mimi had so many questions about the world and had been pretending for so long that Natasha held the answers that she'd become certain that what she pretended was true. Wisdom would speak through her mouth some day. Wisdom, or divine knowledge, or both.

Mimi didn't know what she looked like in her own crown of leaves: the sea never stayed still long enough to use as a mirror.

Once she'd lost her pointer, though, she'd lost interest in sewing. It was too hard to control the needle. And who really cared about crowns? Better to run her remaining fingers through Natasha's curls. Better to whisper stories while Natasha fell asleep. Better to be the only one who could translate Natasha's whimpers, to claim she understood what it meant when the kid gurgled in her sleep. Mimi was waiting for an oracle, for words to pour out through Natasha's little pink bow of a mouth. It would happen. Mimi knew it could happen. She'd spoken once. When she spoke again, Mimi thought, the world would finally make sense. Maybe the pigs would speak through Natasha's mouth. Maybe they would explain what was happening to the world, why the world chose to throw so much away that eventually it would throw enough away to make a new world altogether. Natasha would speak again. She had to. What was the world worth if nobody ever explained it?

She waited for Andrew and Luisa to leave and wondered if this would be the night when the world beyond the world would reveal itself to her.

Otis screamed. They held him down. They laughed when he begged them to stop, when he told them he was a miracle, when he said he'd been born again for a reason and the reason was to help. He screamed and screamed and they clamped their perfumed hands across his mouth until he fell silent. They bound his wrists with rope. They ripped his chain from around his neck. They used gouges, and dropped the dirty gouges on the ground when they were done. They walked away with his eyeballs bleeding in their pockets and they lit cigarettes and poured drinks and said they wished he would stop crying, what a coward, what a baby, too pathetic to call a man.

Andrew and Luisa crept outside at dawn. Their plan was as general as a plan could be: they'd sneak up to the grown-ups' villa, find Otis, set him free, and bring him back. If necessary, once back, they'd hide him. In the faint dawn light, Luisa pressed her hands into her cheeks. She considered their route intently. She mentioned trees they might hide behind, and Andrew agreed. They were both skinny. Neither had bathed in a long time, and a layer of dust coated their arms and legs—they'd fade right into the bark, become nothing more than eyes. Luisa nodded her head. They were in this together.

"Luisa," Andrew whispered just before they left. "Luisa, do you think Otis might have been put here to take care of us?"

"I don't know," Luisa whispered back.

"Do you think someone's paying attention to us from far away? Do you think that's why he's here?"

"I hope so," Luisa said. "I hope so, but I really don't know." She really didn't. She wished she did. Andrew's eyes looked lonely, those big eyes staring into hers, and she wished she had something to offer him.

"Do you really think you'd like a father?" she asked.

"Wouldn't we all?" he said.

"I don't know," she said. "I don't know what it would be like to have a parent."

She'd been trying to imagine ever since Otis arrived. Well, really, she'd been trying to imagine since Eddie tumbled from the barrel and the other children told her he was her twin. That would mean they shared a father and a mother, but she couldn't think what that would mean. She didn't remember anything from a time before. No hand on her forehead when she had a fever. No hip to nestle her head against. She couldn't find a voice singing her lullabies or telling her to eat her greens or snapping at her to straighten up her room. The closest she could come to anything about another world was the way she rubbed her thumb and pointer together just before she fell asleep, or the way she used to, before that pointer was gobbled up. When she'd pressed her fingers together, she'd imagined that what she really felt was the ghost of a baby blanket as soft as a kitten's ear. Someone must have loved her as a baby and given her that blanket. It was just a guess. She had no real way of knowing. And now she didn't even have the finger to access that gesture anymore.

"Why do you think he likes us?" Luisa asked.

"I don't know," Andrew said. "I'm not sure it's even about liking. I think there's something about kids that makes people with any kind of moral streak recognize that we exist outside the realm of like or dislike. I mean, he might not enjoy being around us, but he recognizes that his job is to protect us. I don't even think it's a human thing. I think all animals do it. Maybe it's where humans get to show their most animal side. Maybe what gives us souls is our closeness to animals. Maybe it's the human part of us that's the problem. I don't know."

"I want him back," Luisa said.

"I do too," Andrew said.

"Come on," she said. The two children nodded and set off.

The light from below the horizon was milky. The entire island was quiet. The trees that lined the path looked like ladies in silver dresses. They walked between them, and when they brushed against the leaves, the leaves dropped dew onto their skin.

When they got to the top of the path, the villa rose white in front of them. They hardly ever had a chance to really look at it, just like they hardly ever had a chance to really stare at the grown-ups. But the island was so still now that it was almost telling them to stop, to look. The walls of the villa were built of stone and stucco. Its flat roof was tiled with clay. Vines crept up its whole east wall, and just now opened their pink blossoms to the sun's rising light. Olive trees shaded the wall to the south, and fruit trees grew to the west. The stone patio spread out with views toward the sea, though it was the sea from a different angle than the children ever saw. It was a sea that was sheltered by the island's gentle curve. There was a narrow path that led down to the ocean, and a stone jetty jutted out at its end. They saw a dolphin leap from the water just beyond the jetty. Then they saw a whole pod of dolphins leap in the morning light.

"Do you think it would be possible to get on one of those dolphins' backs and just ride away?" Luisa whispered.

"Where would you go?" Andrew whispered back.

"I don't know. I don't care. Just away from here. Off the island. Look at them. They're playing tag." One dolphin chased the rest, and it moved so fast that the other dolphins didn't stand a chance. They all laughed when it caught them, and then they started over again.

"Look!" Luisa shouted. A dolphin jumped high out of the water, high into the air. It twisted in a circle and then righted itself and dove back in.

"Shh," Andrew said.

"Look at them!" Luisa said. She ran toward the edge of the lawn, stumbled, righted herself, and then crouched down, watching.

"You're being too loud," Andrew said. "They'll hear you." He caught up with her and put his hand on her arm, and when she stepped forward again, he pulled her back.

"Stop it," Luisa said. "Let go."

The dolphin leapt from the water again. The water spraying off its skin caught the light and shimmered. The sun was up a little higher now, and the island birds began to sing.

"Come on," Luisa said. "Let's go down." She could see herself riding on the back of one of those dolphins, streaking through the water, gliding high above it whenever the sea tried to shrug her away. She could feel its smooth skin between her knees, oddly dry even as it emerged from the water. They would move so fast together, so fast that she wouldn't even be able to remember the island they left behind. She didn't know where they would go, but it would take her somewhere safe. Somewhere safe and beautiful and where she'd be happy every minute of every day. It was all clear in her imagination even if her actual vision was blurred.

Just then a hand reached out from the villa and pushed a pair of blue shutters away from a window with a bang.

"You woke them up," Andrew said.

"I did not," Luisa said. She felt her face go red. Of course she'd woken them up. Of course she'd broken any chance they had for stealth.

The two of them ran close to the house, crouching low beneath the window. The world was silent for so long that finally they held their breath and stood on tiptoes and reached up to the window sill to take a look.

The room was a mess. From the window it looked like a dormitory. The floor was covered with crumpled clothes, belts and stockings and lace underwear scattered everywhere. The grown-ups all seemed to have beds of their own, though how many beds exactly it was hard to say. Each bed was draped with a gauzy mosquito netting cloak, but the beds were lined up two by two just like in the juice-stained set of *Madeline* books Luisa had thrown to the pigs the week before. From the window, Luisa and Andrew couldn't see the grown-ups clearly, but they could hear the sounds of their sleepy breathing, and they could see their fancy shoes kicked off beside their beds. Boys and girls seemed to share the same room. Or maybe it was men and women. It was hard to think of the grown-ups as grown up when they slept together like French orphans tucked in matching beds.

Andrew took one look at the room and crouched back on the ground. "Let's get out of here," he said. "Otis must be somewhere else."

Luisa ignored him. She gripped the windowsill and pulled herself up higher, balancing on her arms.

One of the bodies in one of the beds began to stir. First it stretched out sleepy arms to push the netting to the side. Then it kicked covers off sleepy feet. The sheets were bunched up around the middle of the body, and whoever it was, golden hair fell to the body's shoulders. Luisa waited for it to turn toward her so she could see who was waking up. Would it be the one who always wore red lipstick? If so, would she be wearing it now? Would it be the one who twirled the waxed ends of his mustache and wore a cream colored blazer that was always clean, no matter what part of the island he was trekking through? If so, interesting that he didn't actually sleep in the blazer. Maybe it was the one who wore cologne, or the one with pointy teeth, or the one who wore the emerald ring. She screwed up her eyes, but she couldn't make out the details. The stretching of limbs was slow and languorous and for quite some time Luisa thought whoever it was would just go back to sleep. Andrew tugged at her leg and she tried to pull her eyes away—they were there to search for Otis. But she couldn't look away for long: all those sleeping bodies made it impossible to resist turning back. She'd never had a chance to stare at the grown-ups as squarely as she was doing now. They looked like dolls.

When the body finally turned, it wasn't the woman with the lipstick or the man with the mustache, or any of the other grown-ups she had seen before. In fact, it wasn't a grown-up at all. It was Eddie. His eyes were shut, and his lips were slightly parted, and he made small scared sounds in his sleep and moved his hands like he was trying to pull ropes apart. Luisa stared at him and rubbed her eyes, and stared again.

There he was. Sleeping in the same room with the grown-ups. Was there really any difference between a child and an adult?

Eddie's cries turned into humming, and he sighed and nestled his cheek into the pillow, which must have been stuffed with down. Feathers floated in the golden light. His cheek looked soft, and his hair gleamed like threads of spun gold. His lashes were long. They sent fronds of shadows across his cheeks. There was no way he bore a resemblance to Luisa now. If they were twins once, they weren't twins anymore. But how was it possible to be the same once, and then to separate so decisively? It didn't seem right, but maybe she just didn't want it to be possible. Maybe she was confusing the way she wanted the world to be with the way the world actually was. Maybe it was time she recognized the fact that the world rarely presents itself as we expect it to, that it rarely answers anyone's predictions. Luisa shook her head. *Stop*, she told herself. *Just stop.*

When Eddie's eyes fluttered open, Luisa ducked. When Eddie climbed out of bed and reached his naked golden arms out the window to embrace the day, Luisa scooted beneath a bush and pulled Andrew with her. Eddie leaned half his body out. Even the tiny hairs on his arms were gold.

Eddie began to hum for real now, and Luisa recognized the song. It was the same odd tune she hummed sometimes under her breath. She'd been singing it that night in the net. She must have hummed it all night until dawn finally arrived and the grown-ups came. She'd been awake when they'd wrapped their long-nailed fingers tight in Eddie's hair and dragged him, whimpering, from the net. She'd shut her eyes then, but not before she'd seen light flashing and hoped with her eyes shut that the flashes of light came from the rising sun reflecting off silver bracelets and not from the sun reflecting off the sharp steel blades of knives.

"I know you're there," Eddie whispered then. "I can smell you. You should consider taking a bath some time." His voice was cold and smooth and quiet.

Luisa bit her lip. Andrew pressed his hand into hers. They stayed so still that the only thing that moved now was their hearts.

"If I catch you spying again," Eddie whispered, "I'll tear your hair out strand by strand. I'll lock you in a cave in the dark forever. You should be careful."

Luisa stayed as still as she could, but in her heart she was crying, "Sandwich eater! Greedy sandwich eater! We should have fed *you* to the pigs."

"Watch out," Eddie hissed. "That's all I'll say. I have my eye on all of you. On that old man, too. Actually, I don't really need to have my eye on him anymore."

He laughed. And then he pulled his arms back inside and slammed the shutters hard. The bang was so loud it could easily have woken up all the other grown-ups. Would waking them so suddenly put them in a bad mood? Luisa wondered whether she and Andrew should run back to the hut and whether they should spend the day looking for a new cave. Should they hide in a cave in the dark forever? She shivered. She hated the dark. She thought about feeding Eddie to the pigs, and what his screams would sound like, and how quickly he would disappear. She thought about the moment Eddie's screams would fall silent, and about his sharp nailed feet vanishing last. She hated herself for imagining it but she couldn't stop. She wished Eddie had never arrived. She wished his barrel had sunk at sea. She wished they'd pushed him into the pen and turned their backs and walked away.

In the distance, Luisa and Andrew heard a howl. It might have been Otis screaming from an unknown place, or it might just have been the wind sweeping in across the sea.

"Our whole life's garbage," Luisa said. "We should just feed ourselves to the pigs."

Things at the children's hut down below didn't feel quite right that morning. The air was still. The ocean was so calm it looked like silk. Mimi spent the morning pacing back and forth, shading her eyes to look up the path, and then pacing even faster when each time she looked there was nothing there. Occasional screams. Occasional moans that started quiet and rose to hurricane-force howls. Then silence. No Luisa. No Andrew. Not even any unusual shadows shifting across the path. Finally, she hoisted herself into the leafy arms of the tree that stood at the bottom of the hill and leaned back in the cool shade and covered her ears with her hands so if the screaming started again she might not hear it.

The tree stretched its branches out right above the pigs. It was crazy that Andrew hadn't discovered it yet. He climbed everything else, but he was scared of the pigs; she knew he was scared even when he pretended that he wasn't. He didn't have the guts to climb into branches that spread out over their pen. Mimi wasn't scared. There was no way she would ever fall.

She was sick of watching for Andrew and Luisa. Where were they? She was just going to sit up there in the branches and look at the ocean. They didn't need her worry to help them come back.

She took her hands off her ears. Silence.

Natasha was driving Mimi crazy. It was like the kid was a duckling who thought Mimi was her mother. She followed her everywhere, watching her with her big, silent eyes. She shoved her head in Mimi's lap whenever Mimi sat down. She tossed her head back and forth until Mimi played with her ringlets, and those ringlets smelled. Natasha refused to take a bath, no matter how perfect the water was, no matter how many toys they fashioned from their forks and spoons and plates and bowls to put in the water with her, no matter how many stories they told her about dirty children turning into pigs; she wouldn't climb into the barrel they used as a tub. And of course she'd never say why. That was the worst—the silence. And the smell. When it came to Natasha, Mimi knew the grown-ups were right: the children did smell. Maybe noticing meant she wasn't a child anymore.

If the kid would just talk, she thought. If the kid would talk things might be different. "It's him." That was all she'd ever said. It had seemed so important, like finally there was a reason for the silence and a reason for the breaking of the silence. It had seemed like there was wisdom, somewhere, and that it spoke through the lips of a little girl. But all she did was whine incoherently now. And, really, they could have figured out it was Eddie without her help.

Mimi wished there were a boy her own age, or maybe just a little older, on the island. She wished they could sneak off and walk, holding hands, even injured hands, along the coast. She wished she knew what it felt like to have another person's lips pressed against her own.

It was unfair that the only child to arrive in ages was Eddie. Sure, he was Luisa's brother, and they probably should have taken better care of him for that reason alone, but he hadn't been the right age to be of real interest to Mimi when he'd arrived, and he didn't have any of the redeeming qualities that his sister had—though at this moment, her bad mood and worry taking over everything, Mimi couldn't quite remember what Luisa's redeeming qualities were. She was always running off and falling down. Mimi was sick of hearing her talk about getting off the island. It would never happen. Eddie had smelled nearly as bad as Natasha when he came out of that barrel. He'd needed a shower. Not that any of them would ever have access to a shower. Mimi dreamed of a private bathroom like the ones she saw in discarded magazine after discarded magazine, where she could shower for hours and keep her makeup supplies in private drawers that no one else pawed through. She dreamed of having makeup supplies in general. She ate up tattered advertisements for mascara almost as ravenously as the pigs ate dreams.

She'd thought for a very short time that Otis might help them. She almost laughed now. That old man, broken, disgusting, really, with his empty locket around his neck. His fingernails alone made her gag. What had he done for them? Leaving in the middle of the night, forcing Andrew and Luisa to go look for him. All he'd done was make her lonelier. She wished he'd never emerged from the sea.

She heard another scream. She put her hands back up over her ears, but it didn't help at all.

The pigs paid attention to details. They knew she climbed the tree. When she'd first started doing it, years ago, they'd sat back like dogs and howled up at her like they were howling at the moon. But they'd gotten used to her above, and sometimes she dropped books down to them, old paperbacks that people threw away instead of sending to Goodwill. She kept a supply of them under her pillow and read them secretly when the other kids were outside. She'd read anything. Cookbooks. Phonebooks. Math workbooks that had all the problems filled out. Now the pigs waited patiently for the pages to rain down. It was fun feeding them from above. They opened their mouths and smiled. Their skin glistened in the light. They were especially beautiful from that angle.

Mimi was ashamed, but she sometimes wished she could spend more time with the grown-ups. She wanted to know where they got their clothes. She wanted to know how they kept their skin so smooth. They could tell her how to fix her stringy hair. They could teach her about which hand should hold a fork and which should hold a knife. Her face flushed thinking about it—just the thought of wanting to be one of the grown-ups felt like a betrayal. Why couldn't a book ever wash ashore that would teach her, step by step, how best to become an adult?

Andrew and Luisa had been gone so long now that it seemed like they were never coming back. A heavy stillness settled over the island. Natasha had moved inside the hut and was whimpering from within its walls, but give her two minutes and she'd drop into sleep. Mimi leaned her head back, and took her hands off her ears, and stretched out against the long branch, and looked up at the green leaves, and pretended that she was happy. She fiddled with a leaf.

These were the sounds that she could hear when she finally listened:

The sea slapping against trash in a methodical way, shrugging it onto shore and patting it in place so it didn't wash back out.

The pigs rehearsing a lullaby, crooning softly in the shade.

A dove, out in the hills, cooing again and again.

The rasp of cicadas, roused, surprisingly and suddenly, from more than a decade of sleep.

Natasha wailing inside the hut, wordless, slobbery—probably crying for Mimi, but really crying for a mother. Mimi wasn't her mother. She was too young. *Please*, she thought sometimes, *please, somebody remember that I'm too young to have a child*. Natasha needed to learn how to talk. Even if it wasn't to predict the future or explain why life was the way it was she at least had to learn how to make her needs known with the specificity that words allow. It was just unfair to everyone else around her otherwise. The wailing of a wordless child was too much to bear.

Mimi's own thoughts were loudest of all, rattling and rattling around in her head.

I just want some quiet, she thought. Actually, she said it aloud, but not loud enough for anyone to hear. Just loud enough to notice how strange her own voice sounded. Like it was coming from someone else's lips.

She sat up again and looked at the garbage heaped on the shore.

There were plastic sandwich bags with half eaten salami sandwiches, and shoes from Kmart that had never fit anyway and were tossed into the garbage with their tags still on. There were peace treaties in broken frames, covered in ketchup from the tons and tons of single serving packets that get thrown away with empty bags of fries. There was advice that came whispering ashore, the words of parents to their teenage children—*use protection. Make sure he loves you. There's nothing wrong with waiting*. There were cars that had worked until they'd hit their 200,000 mile mark, and then had just turned over once more and died. There were bathtubs that no one realized could be re-enameled, and hypodermic needles that really *should* be thrown away and were exactly where they belonged. There was spaghetti and sauce left over from all-you-can-eat spaghetti dinners. There were birth control provisions from health care plans, and moldy rice, and moldy bread, and moldy cheese that was intended to be moldy and had been thrown away by mistake. The ocean groaned. The island smelled. The pigs lumbered up from their places in the shade and paced back and forth frantically. It looked like there was so much to consume that they had no idea where to begin, and without the children there to bring it to them, they had no method to reach it anyway.

Mimi gritted her teeth and thought about Otis. She was glad he'd vanished. She hoped the screams she'd heard were his. Who knew why the pigs didn't eat him. Looking out at the refuse heaping itself on the shore, it was clearer than ever to Mimi that Otis had simply gotten separated from his shipment. Besides being human, what was the difference between him and any of the other discards in the mess washing up from the sea? What did the pigs know that she didn't? Sometimes even giant, magic pigs made mistakes.

The dove cooing in the trees upped its volume. Mimi wondered if the season had changed, and the dove was responding to something in nature that she couldn't see. She couldn't remember hearing it before, but since Otis arrived, it seemed as though every time she shut her eyes and tried to think, there was that dove cooing as if to say, "Remember me? Take heart." She would gladly have shot it with an arrow and roasted it over a fire for dinner. There was no way she'd be able to handle a bow with her missing fingers, but still. Given the chance, she would do it.

She knew what she was supposed to do. Other kids or not, she should get to work. The garbage was easier to handle when they worked as a team, but really—and this was something she'd only come to lately—life on the island was a solo exercise. Sometimes you had company and sometimes you didn't. It was best to realize you were in this world alone. But she was tired, and the garbage smelled, and the last thing she wanted to do was pick through it piece by piece and toss all those pieces over the fence to the frantic jaws of the pigs.

"I don't want to be a child anymore," she said.

The pigs were silent for a moment.

The dove was silent for a moment.

For a second, the ocean held its panicked breath.

She reached down and picked up an almost empty tube of lipstick. She smeared it across her lips. "The world can't force me to work," she shouted out to the sea. "I refuse."

The pigs shook their heads, and resumed their pacing.

The dove started up again. Who knew why it had stopped.

The ocean heaved and shrugged, and a flock of elderly chickens squawked onto the shore.

When Mimi looked down at the ground, it seemed slightly farther away than usual. When she looked up at the branches of the tree, they looked slightly closer. Her dress felt different, and she realized she must have grown real breasts without noticing. The threadbare fabric barely made it over her hips. She rubbed her wrist across her mouth and it came back smudged with pink.

"I'm leaving," she whispered.

She waited for the island's reaction, but this time there was no response.

"I'm sorry," she whispered. "I'm going to figure out a way."

She stepped into the hut to grab her things, and just as she did, Natasha opened up her eyes and opened her mouth and spoke.

Natasha's voice was sweet and clear. "I want more," she said. "I want more."

The distance between now and when the pigs first arrived was impossible to calculate. For millions of years their meals were few and far between. There wasn't much garbage to be had for most of those years, and what there was, was mostly emotional. They nibbled on broken hearts and exiled kings, but everything in households was mostly used and reused until it turned to dust, and what wasn't used was buried close to home. Forget about clothes gone out of fashion. Forget about plastic. There wasn't any excess. The pigs didn't even realize they were hungry.

Somewhere along the way, though, things started changing. Who knows exactly what caused the change—what was it that prompted someone to start wrapping goods in paper? Maybe the age of exploration? Maybe the Industrial Revolution? Whatever it was, one day some moldy biscuit washed ashore, and then a bolt of cloth, and then furniture abandoned along the Oregon Trail. When plastic was invented the stream turned into a river.

The pigs ate almost constantly now. Good thing they never got full. Sometimes their jaws ached from overuse, but they were ravenous, always.

Up at the villa, the cost of choices made was clearer than it was down by the water. Andrew and Luisa crouched behind the bush, too scared to make a run for it. They heard shutters slam against the sides of the building. They heard grumpy morning conversation, and they smelled coffee, and they heard a quiet kind of crying in the background. And then, just when they told themselves they should move or get caught, just when Luisa said she couldn't stand crouching anymore, just when Andrew nodded his head in agreement, just when they stood up to run but realized their bodies were cramped from all that cowering on cold ground, a hand that might as well have been disembodied reached out and grabbed them and marched them by their ears around the edge of the building and through the villa's entryway.

An hour later they were pressed down on the marble floor, kneeling in front of an enormous case of silverware. Eddie looked down on them, impassive, like a golden statue. His long nails occasionally scraped their arms. They polished spoons and polished forks, but nothing would come clean. Spots of tarnish formed again as soon as the polishing cloth moved on. Eddie sat on a chair that looked like a throne and cracked a whip from time to time and rapped his scepter on the floor.

"I want these pieces shining," he said. "I want to see my own reflection in these knives."

Luisa knew she shouldn't look at him. She knew they'd be safer if she just did her job and pretended she wasn't there. But she couldn't help herself, and each time she looked up, ready with a scowl on her face, he hit her.

The world of the hut and the world of the villa merged here where Andrew and Luisa's bony knees hit the cold marble floor. They polished and polished and polished, and when Luisa thought Eddie wasn't looking, she spat on the silverware in spite. Her shoulders hurt and her back hurt. Her elbows hurt and her knees hurt. Her toes cramped from the pressure on them when she tilted her body back to survey the size of the silverware case. It was as big as a coffin. Their work would never be done, but if by some crazy chance they did finish, what would happen to them then? The sun through the open door was so hot and her throat was so dry that she ultimately stopped spitting because she didn't have the fluids for it. Throughout it all, Eddie took long sips of lemonade.

It was like standing in front of a door in a windowless room, but a door that has sealed itself back into the wall so that the room is without entrance or exit. It was like riding an elevator with buttons that have vanished so there is no way of choosing a floor to make it stop. It was like there was no color with enough pigment to describe the pain.

The world knocked into him whenever he moved. It was like it was all elbows jabbing in the gut. It was like it was all hallways too narrow to squeeze through. It was like it was water and he was thirst and there was no cup to bring the world to his lips.

It was like his eyes were empty stomachs and the earth had stopped producing food. It was like his eyes were empty stomachs and his mouth had been severed from his face.

The door to the windowless room remained shut and Otis's fingers bled from trying to find its frame.

Andrew went to the pump to fill the empty bucket. The water got dirty quickly and the pail was heavy each time he brought clean water back. His shoulders ached. Water sloshed out of the bucket and against his legs. It itched as it trickled down his skin. He wished Eddie had died that night in the net. He wished he had stayed with Otis where he'd found him, just the two of them on Otis's beach. Luisa had come to help, but look what she'd done. Every instinct she'd ever had was wrong. He couldn't help blaming her for getting them caught.

Once full, the bucket took everything he had to lift. Flies buzzed around his ears but he didn't have a hand free to swat them with.

He was carrying the fifth refill back when he heard a loud sobbing from behind the bush closest to the pump. The plant was an oleander with spiky leaves and magenta buds just opening, and the leaves and flowers together made a dense web. The flowers were so bright they seemed to vibrate. When he looked, he found Otis. Who was missing his eyeballs. And beside himself with grief. He'd wedged himself up against the bush and had his knees to his chest and his shoulders shook and he twined a broken chain through his fingers and pressed its metal locket against his lips.

Andrew retched. He had to lean against the pump to keep himself from falling. Thick blood oozed down Otis's cheeks.

"Otis?" Andrew said. "What did they do to you?"

Otis sucked in his breath.

"Andrew?" he said. "Is that you?"

"It's me," Andrew said. "What did they do to you?"

"Andrew," Otis said. "Be careful. These people are bad. Why would they hurt me like this?"

Otis's arms, each wrist wrapped in rope, were tied in front of him. The flies that had circled around Andrew's ears settled in Otis's empty sockets. He shook his head and they lifted in a cloud, then settled again as soon as he was still.

"I'm blind, Andrew. I'm blind," he moaned. "Where is the world? I can't see it anywhere."

His face was all shadows and absence. His eyes were empty caves. Andrew's stomach turned again. His heart beat against its cage, and there were tears on his cheeks that he didn't even know had come from his own seeing eyes.

"How will I get home without my eyes?" Otis wailed. The ends of the ropes that bound his wrists were shredded, as though he'd been trying to work them loose with his teeth. Scrapes covered his arms. A chain-patterned bruise wrapped around his neck. A bloody gash striped his left shoulder. His right ankle bulged as if it had a tennis ball inside it. "Who will save me?" he cried. "When will someone rescue me?"

Andrew took Otis's arm and pulled him to his feet. He swatted flies away. They rose in a swarm from Otis's skin and settled on the oleander blossoms beside him, and then lifted up again and settled back upon his head.

Andrew looked to make sure no one was watching. Then he led Otis to the path that wound around the villa and back down toward the children's hut. He gave him a little push and told him to keep walking. The flies were like a crown around his head.

"Look for Mimi," Andrew said. "Tell her where we are. Tell her she should take you and run."

"I can't look," Otis said. "I won't ever be able to look again."

"Then you'll have to feel your way to her," Andrew said. "You'll find her."

Otis moved off, nodding, limping, broken and old and horrible, barely able to stay on the path, his locket pressed to his mouth like it was the only thing he believed was real. The flies moved with him as if they were the clouds of his own personal storm. When he stopped occasionally to catch his breath, the sucking in was like the wind.

Luisa had been down on her knees on the wet marble for hours. Andrew came and went and came and went with the bucket of water. She wanted a chance at that bucket, but Eddie flicked his whip whenever she tried to stand up. "You stay here until I say you can move," he said. "The only thing you're good for is cleaning up my mess." She felt like she would collapse on that marble floor and die.

She got a small break whenever Andrew was gone to fetch clean water, or, if not a break, at least she got a chance to dry out. Her hands were so tender from working with wet rags that the skin was starting to peel away from her nails. Her knees looked like raw meat. Her throat was incredibly dry. Now it seemed like he'd been gone forever, and she looked at her knees and wondered if they'd ever heal.

"Stop complaining," Eddie said. "You act like this is the worst thing that could happen to you, but think about what it would be like to wake up in a net with knives held to your throat. Think about what things have been like for me."

"When is Andrew coming back?" Luisa said.

"Who cares about Andrew," Eddie said. "Why don't you ever pay attention to me?" He flicked his wrist and the whip snapped and she felt it tear a strip of skin away from her neck. She yelped. She curled her hand into a fist. He laughed. "You should see my closet," he said. "It's fantastic. It's better than anything I had back home."

"I don't care about your closet," Luisa said. She said it under her breath, but still, there was no way for him not to hear. He flicked the whip again, and she yelped again, and she rubbed her fist across her forehead, and when she pulled it away it was smeared with blood, and she looked up at him and glared.

"You act like all of this is my fault," Eddie said. "You're the one who didn't think about anything except saving yourself. What did you think would happen? Were you hoping they'd kill me? Look at me."

Luisa looked at him. He was skinny, and his torso was bare, and she could see his ribs. His hand grasped the whip like he didn't know what else to hold onto.

"I'm so sorry I didn't try to keep you safe," she said.

"It's a little late for sorry," Eddie said.

"I mean it," Luisa said. "I wasn't thinking, there inside the net. I always do things without thinking. If I could go back and change what I did, I would. I really would."

He tapped the handle of the whip against his knee. He looked like he was figuring something out. "Do you want to see where we keep the clothes?" he said.

Luisa turned her head to see if he was talking to someone else. No one else was there. "The clothes?"

"My closet. Like I said, it's pretty great. Come on. Andrew's taking forever to bring that water back. We'll have fun."

"I'm not interested in clothes," Luisa said.

Eddie's face fell. But it brightened again quickly. "How about the pantry then? I'll show you where we keep the sweets."

Luisa didn't want to go. She wanted Andrew to come back, and she wanted to take his hand and run away. But she'd said no once and she was afraid to say it again. Blood ran down her cheek. She wiped it away and nodded.

Eddie took her arm. He led her through the villa. They walked past the ballroom and past the bedroom. They passed a marble staircase and beyond that they walked down a hall with doors on either side. Eventually Eddie opened a door on the sea-facing side of the villa and they stepped into what must have been the pantry. The walls were lined with shelves. On each shelf were trays of fresh baked pastries set aside to cool.

"Who makes these?" Luisa said.

Eddie shrugged. "Who cares? What matters is what they taste like." He took a cream puff off a tray and shoved it whole inside his mouth. His cheeks bulged and it took a while to chew it up. When he finally was able to swallow, he had a smear of yellow cream smudged across his bottom lip.

"Delicious," he said.

Luisa nodded and looked around the room. There were rows of tarts piled with berries and covered with a glaze that made them shine as bright as jewels. There were éclairs dripping with chocolate and napoleons etched with frosting patterns that looked like feathers and macarons in every color Luisa had ever seen. The far side of the room was filled with custard: bowls of ice cream that miraculously stayed frozen despite the temperature of the room which, while not hot, was certainly not as cold as ice cream needs to remain intact; cups of pudding; flattened pyramids of flan; ramekins of creme brûlée. Water pooled inside her mouth. She'd never tried anything like what was on those shelves but she knew by instinct that she'd feel like she was dying, in a good way, if she could try just one.

"The raspberry tarts are my favorite," Eddie said. He lifted one up and took a large bite. Powdered sugar puffed up and settled on his nose. He chewed and chewed and then looked at her. "We're going to serve them at my party. You should come. It's happening tonight. You could sit next to me. Try one." He waved at the shelf. Luisa swallowed. "Any one you want," he said. "I'm sharing. See, I know how to share."

Luisa's hand crept out on its own. She looked down and there it was, reaching for an éclair. The pastry was soft. She squeezed it slightly. Her other hand reached out and ran a finger over the chocolate frosting and then popped the finger in her mouth. She'd never had chocolate before. She thought her knees would give way.

"I love éclairs," Eddie said. "I love how soft they are. I love the cream inside."

Luisa nodded. She brought the pastry to her mouth and she could smell the sweet flour and the chocolate and she opened her mouth and took a bite.

It's hard to imagine being moved enough by a pastry to think about changing one's entire path in life. A poem might do it, or an article in the newspaper, or a chance encounter with a stranger on the subway, but a pastry? Sweets are sweets—who cares? Luisa knew while she was chewing that the perfect marriage of taste and texture shouldn't mean so much to her, but who's to judge? She felt like she'd do anything to just keep eating éclairs every day for the rest of her life.

"You can stay with me," Eddie said. "I'll find a bed for you. I'll get you a bath. Someone can style your hair and you won't believe how good you'll look. You can eat as much as you want and sleep as much as you want and we'll be best friends *and* brother and sister. I'm so lonely here."

Luisa nodded. She had her eyes shut and was focusing on the taste. She wanted to try a blueberry tart with lemon curd as soon as she was done. And then after that she thought she'd try a salted caramel macaron, and then a pistachio macaron, and then an ice cream sundae.

"I've been a little lonely," Eddie said. "It's hard to admit, but I think the reason I've been so angry is because I'm scared of ending up alone. I'm so glad you're here with me. Maybe we could even go down to the beach from time to time to visit the other kids. We need them to keep working, but there's nothing to stop us from visiting."

Luisa nodded again. After the sundae she thought she'd go back to pastry. Maybe try a napoleon. Maybe try something simple like a brownie. Something with chocolate. She couldn't get enough chocolate. She opened her eyes and Eddie was looking at her with the first real smile she'd ever seen on his face and she shut her eyes again and wondered if she was dreaming.

And then she heard the sound of a grown man sobbing. There weren't any windows in that shelf-lined room, and it was difficult to tell where the sound was coming from. It was so loud, though, that it practically shook the walls. And it was clearly a man. And he was clearly in deep pain. For a moment, Luisa's teeth ground together. And then her stomach felt slightly sick. She opened her eyes. Eddie was still smiling, and she wondered if he could hear what she heard.

"We'll toast marshmallows and make s'mores," he said. "We'll eat *al fresco* tonight and then we'll play catch."

"I don't think so," Luisa said. She put the plate with the half-eaten blueberry tart back on the shelf. "I have to get back to help Andrew."

"No," Eddie said.

"I have to," Luisa said.

The sobbing continued, and she was sure that Eddie could hear it. He was just ignoring it, the way he was trying to get her to ignore everything that mattered.

"Just stay here a little while with me," Eddie said. "I'll run a bath for you. I'll have 800–thread count sheets put on your bed. We'll have a great time at the party."

"Are you crazy?" Luisa said. "Can't you hear that sound?"

"What sound?" Eddie said. "Why don't you like me? Why don't any of the kids like me?"

"You whipped me," Luisa said. "You make up stupid, horrible jobs for us to do. You live up here and you don't care about what's happening anywhere besides exactly where you are. You're a pig yourself, but the bad kind. The kind that wrecks everything. The kind that makes everything into a mess instead of cleaning it up. Why would we like you?"

The sobbing turned into a kind of hiccupy gulping. Without thinking, Luisa stepped out of the little pantry and slammed the door shut behind her. She pulled a bolt to lock it tight. And then she ran. She could hear Eddie hammering from behind the door. The sobs outside were so loud that she didn't think anyone would hear him pounding for a while. Maybe he would be trapped inside the pantry forever. Just then, she didn't care. She raced down the hallway and down the steps and through the foyer and smacked right into Andrew as soon as she got out the door.

Otis stumbled down the path by himself in darkness.
The world. The sea. The sun. Shadows. Shapes.
Edges. Shades. Where were they?

Always, always he'd known there was more to the world than he could see, but now there was nothing to see and he didn't want the invisible world. It was no consolation at all. He wanted the world through his eyes.

Why wasn't the world storming around him? How could the winds not rise to match his heart?

Otis tripped, then righted himself, but he'd twisted his already swollen ankle and now, along with everything else, he limped. He seemed to fall in every hole there was. Every part of his body felt broken.

"Isn't there anyone watching?" he raged. "Isn't there anyone who cares?"

No one listened. Or maybe they did, but without being able to see he had no way of knowing if anyone was there.

"I need shelter," he shouted. "There's a storm coming and I need somewhere to hide."

The flies buzzed in circles around his head. They landed on his brow and on his nose and just below his empty bleeding sockets. He could feel their tiny feet and the vibrations of their wings. He batted them away, and they circled and landed once again. He wiped his hand across his face. When it came away sticky he didn't know if the stickiness was sweat or blood or both. He hurt deeper in his body than he thought was possible.

"Here I am," he yelled. "I'm waiting to be rescued."

He'd thought the pigs had spared him so he could save the children. He'd made a choice to intervene. Why had he made a choice when he'd always been exactly the kind of person who avoided making choices? He hadn't even thought about it as defending—more as inserting a voice of reason where no reason seemed to be at work. He should have focused on getting a message to his family. Or better yet, he should have drowned in the ocean. He wished he'd drowned. Better to fall under a blanket of water than to fall to the cruelty of human hands. Why couldn't the pigs have eaten him when they'd had the chance?

He'd wasted so much time. There was so much to look at in the world. There was so much he'd never look at again. He knew the world best through his eyes. How could he ever know the world again?

He must have been close to the hut. He could still feel the ghost of Andrew's hands on his back. When he reached the hut, would there be anyone there waiting for him? What would Alice think of him? He wanted to see her gray eyes one more time. He wanted to fall to his knees and press his face into the dirt and die. Would anyone make him stand up again if he collapsed right here? Could anyone? He was disappointing, weak, hated by everything he couldn't see and everything that could see him without him even knowing. Where were his eyes now? What was out there for him if he couldn't see?

He fell to his knees, and the flies bit the tips of his ears and the back of his neck. He stumbled up again and they moved away from his skin, circling. Maybe like a crown. Maybe like a halo. He couldn't see the swarm, but their

buzzing was steady as they circled, and he felt their movement like a twister around his head.

His legs hurt. His knees hurt. His face throbbed. His
head pounded. His eyes, where he should have hurt the
most, felt empty, and his heart felt empty, and the world felt
empty too. He had been his eyes. Now he was an absence.

The flies lifted, circled, landed.

Just then, it almost felt as though the flies were flicking
their wings to fan his skin.

He reached the hut and stumbled to the door. He fell to
the ground and wept without tears and the door in front of
him opened and he felt a small girl's hands on his head.

"I want a mother," Natasha said. Her hands cupped Otis's bloody face. "I want someone to feed me with a spoon. I want a kitten. I want a pony. I want a tame squirrel or at least a chipmunk.

"Couldn't I get my nails done? Couldn't I get my ears pierced? It doesn't cost much—I could wear gold studs for a year.

"I'd like a jar of fireflies. I'd like French toast for breakfast every day. I'd like leg of lamb for lunch. But only if we have rosemary. And only if you promise not to make me try mint jelly.

"I want my own bedroom. I want my own bathroom. I want ten new pairs of shoes."

Her hands were soft. Her knees were chubby. Her breath smelled like milk. There was an endless list of things she wanted, and her voice rang with the clearness of a bell.

Mimi stared at her, not believing this was what she'd waited for.

Otis collapsed in the doorway and, with his face in the dirt, he wept and wept and wept.

An hour later, Otis could sense the boards of the hut above his head. They were too low for a man his size. The dirt floor was hard. His bones felt like they were close to breaking through his skin, each part unyielding inside of him—his hips, his knees, his elbows. His skin barely held his bones together.

This is what you get for trying to help, he thought. A world of darkness, a world of closed-off space. It would be better never even to try.

He'd always been a man of action, if not a man of choice. Even when he was a boy he couldn't sit still. His mother used to tell him to slow down at least five times a day. He'd always felt like there was somewhere to go. He'd carved shapes out of sticks. He'd shoveled snowy walks. He'd mown the front yard without complaining. If he was moving, even if it was just his fingers tapping out a rhythm on the kitchen table, his body felt right.

But now, now all was stillness and pain.

From time to time the oldest girl—Mimi? The teenager?—opened the door and asked him if he needed anything. He had nothing to say. She should be able to look at him and see that the last thing he needed was a child's help. What good were children to a broken man? Anyway, her voice didn't sound like she really meant it when she asked.

He tried to stand. He got dizzy immediately and dropped back down to the ground. He couldn't figure out how to orient himself without his eyes. It was like swim-

ming where—underwater and afraid to open your eyes—
you sometimes lose track of which way is up.

He slid down the wall and pressed his cheek into the
earthen floor. He realized he was gripping his broken locket and he let it slide onto the ground. Who cared about an
empty locket? Who cared about anything? The pigs were
running back and forth so fast that he could feel a tremor in
the ground. There was so much he'd like to feed them. Forget about the bounced checks. Forget about the Hummel
figurines he'd tossed into boxes when he'd moved his mother to a home. What he'd like to feed the pigs were the hours
he'd wasted watching television, the times he'd snapped at
his son for calling for a drink of water when he should have
been asleep, the times when he said he had to be alone when
he really wanted more than anything to be close to another
person. He wanted to tear his heart out of his chest and carry it outside and toss it over the fence to the pigs.

He was too tired to cry. He was too tired to sleep. He lay
on the floor and missed his child, and missed his wife, and
missed the possibilities that weren't possibilities anymore.

From a distance, the question is, why didn't the children go into hiding right away? The question is more easily asked than answered. Why don't any of us do what we know we really should do? Why do we put off until tomorrow what should be done today? Certainly Mimi was horrified by Otis's eyes. Certainly she understood that something about the regular daily violence of that place had shifted. Certainly she wished the latest load of trash contained a book that she could skim through that would tell her what kind of behavior was expected of her. But there were no books tucked in the backpacks with broken zippers that washed up on shore. And Otis didn't say anything. He sat inside the hut and sobbed, and every time he started talking sobs took over again and his voice just disappeared. It was hard to get enough perspective to figure out what to do. She had no access to distance. She spent the entire day hauling trash from shore to pen, avoiding Otis inside the hut, avoiding Natasha, who, now that she could talk, would not stop talking. She waited for Andrew and Luisa to come back down the path. She was worried about them. She was worried about everything.

When dusk began to settle, the three at the hut hadn't taken a step closer to hiding.

And Andrew and Luisa? They never made it even as far as the top of the path. By the time Luisa ran full speed out the villa's door, tripped on the steps, and banged right into Andrew, a couple of grown-ups were scattered across the lawn playing croquet, blocking any access to the path. Ice cubes clinked in glasses and bats swooped through the half-lit sky. Eddie's hammering in the pantry turned into loud screams of rage, and then it turned into a kind of keening, and then it fell into silence. The two children huddled behind a bush and waited for their chance to make a break.

And then the entire island was clothed in darkness, and a party started on the terrace, and Andrew and Luisa were just about to use the cover of darkness to run, when torches burst aflame over by the terrace, and they were drawn to the flickering light like moths flapping their erratic way across a porch, the light turning into everything, the blind man Andrew had sent below as warning becoming as pale to them as any other faded dream.

Mimi knew she should be doing something for Otis, something for them all—packing their clothes? Gathering supplies for what seemed like might be months of hiding? She knew disaster loomed. But all she wanted was to have a moment to herself. Just as the sun began to set, she left Otis crumpled on the hut's earthen floor and Natasha pretending she was wearing high heeled shoes. She ran up the path, turned off it quickly, and pushed her way through bushes toward the interior of the island.

She passed groves of lemon trees that made the air smell like the sun even though the day had almost turned to dark. She passed ancient olive trees, their branches thick as grown men's waists, their silvery leaves catching what was left of the fading light. She passed large granite rocks that looked like ships in a wide green sea. She stopped at one of the rocks, breathing hard, leaning her back against its cool stone face. She just wanted silence. She just wanted to be able to hear herself breathe.

Leaves stirred. Crackling sounds burst from bushes. The sun, shooting its last rays over the horizon, shifted. The rock turned momentarily warm, and she sighed in the dying light and listened to birds.

Eventually she heaved herself on top of the rock. It really was like a ship. She could stand at the tip of its bow and see the ocean glinting far, far below along the edges of the island. Was that the children's hut? If it was bright day she'd be able to tell, but for now she could only guess. If it was, what a perfect place to watch it from afar. She could see tree-tops shifting in the breeze like water. The granite spreading out around her was solid but it seemed to float.

From down below—how far? Ten feet? Fifteen feet? On top of that rock she imagined she was flying—a new sound came. There was a scuffling from some of the bushes. And a kind of hiccupy sucking in of breath. And then, she could see it from above even though the evening light had turned to purple and was really almost gone, the bushes parted and a boy stepped into the clearing.

She knew immediately that it was Eddie. She dropped down on her stomach and stayed completely still. She watched him reach his hand out to touch the rock's rough wall. She watched him lean his body up against the rock and sag against it, pressing his cheek against its heft. He lifted his hands and folded them on top of his head and even from above she could see that his fingers were scratched and bloody. He looked like he'd been prying the lock off a cage. The purple light made his skin look soft. She wondered what it would feel like to touch him, whether his arms would hold heat the way the rock held heat where she lay.

She could hear him whispering to himself in between his sobs. "She left me," she heard. "I was being nice to her. I didn't want to hurt anyone. I really didn't. Nobody came to save me."

She could mostly see his back, the way it heaved and shook as he cried. She wondered if he would stop crying if she ran her hand along his shoulders, along the smooth surface of his face.

"I'm all alone," she heard. "I don't belong anywhere. I'm stuck on the outside watching. Nobody ever comes to help me."

"Don't cry," she found herself calling.

He looked up. He used his arm to wipe away his tears. His wrecked hands left blood on his cheeks. He had some kind of cream smudged on his bottom lip. She wanted to cup his face in her hands and wet a washcloth and clean him up and wipe away his tears and bandage up his hands. Dark was falling, and it was getting hard to see. She brushed her hair away from her eyes. He looked at her. He frowned.

"This is my rock," he said. "What are you doing at my rock?"

"Nothing," Mimi said. "I'm just sitting here."

"You were spying on me," he said. His mouth set. "You were listening to me."

She slid down the rock wall and landed hard on her feet.

"Don't cry," she said again. She reached her hand out and touched his shoulder. His skin was so smooth.

"I wasn't crying," he said. "I'm too old to cry."

"No you're not," she said.

"I am," he said. He pushed her hand away. "And if you tell anyone you saw me crying, you'd better watch out. Actually, you'd better watch out anyway. All of you. I won't forget what you did. You pretend to be so innocent and such hard workers, but when push comes to shove, you take the easy way out. Just like everyone else. I won't forget. She called me a pig. I'll show her a pig."

He turned his back and pushed his way through the bushes. Mimi watched him go. She shivered. Then she turned too, and ran down the path, the dusk having turned so nearly into dark that she worried it would be impossible to find her way home.

It was easy to get close. Andrew and Luisa moved from tree to tree, sliding across the lawn as if they were shadows themselves. The patio was lit with torches. The air smelled of smoke and citronella. The grown-ups lounged against the walls, silhouetted in the light, their gowns long, their pants tight, their strong arms crooked through delicate elbows. Champagne fizzed up in flutes. Paving stones shimmered in the firelight. Luisa's hands throbbed in memory of every wine stain she'd scrubbed out of those stones. Her knees ached in memory of bleach. But that patio—it was so clean it looked like the grown-ups were walking on snow.

"A toast," they heard. A red-haired woman wearing a sequined dress that spread out on the floor like water raised her glass. "A toast to our darling boy."

"A toast," a man wearing a white tuxedo echoed. His mustache swept down along the edges of his mouth like a drawn back velvet curtain. His white teeth gleamed.

"Where is he?" they heard. Grown-ups turned their heads this way and that.

"Has anybody seen him?" A grown-up held her cigarette lighter up high. Another crouched down as if he thought he might find what he was looking for between the long legs around him.

"He took a walk," the red-haired woman said. "I saw him run out through the back door. I think his hands were bleeding. Should we be worried?"

"Oh, here he is. Silly us. He's here!"

Eddie emerged from somewhere, rubbing what looked like dirt off his cheek and then holding his face up as though it were covered with a mask. He wore gloves. They reached his elbows. He walked smoothly. He sat very straight when he settled in a chair, and the adults looked at him adoringly. All chattering paused while the toast was made. He set his mouth in a thin straight line. Then he turned down its outside corners and frowned.

"Don't be sad," the sequined lady said. "Tonight is about celebrating you. We were dying of boredom. We were dying, and you came to us. Our boy."

"You know just what to say when we need to hear something said," the mustachioed man declared.

"You're young, but not like a child," a woman dressed in red velvet sang. Her hair was knotted in a bun at the nape of her neck. She waved her champagne in the air. "You're young in a way I like."

"Yes, youth," cried the mustachioed man. He ran his hand over Eddie's shoulder. "There's nothing wrong with youth."

"I almost want to eat you," the sequined lady said. "You're so delicious. Or maybe I'd rather drink you. You're like a tall drink of water."

Luisa tried to stand. Andrew pulled her back. He reached his hand out and put it around hers. He squeezed hard on her fingers. She nodded. They both bit their bottom lips.

Eddie raised his glass, and all the grown-ups raised their glasses. His torso gleamed in the candlelight. When he spoke, his voice didn't even shake.

"To my real family," he said. "To those I love. To those who stand by me no matter what."

He tipped the glass toward his mouth. The champagne glowed like gold in the light. When he finished drinking he set his mouth in a way that was clear he wanted more.

Music started. Two grown-ups grabbed each other and tangoed across the floor. One carried a rose in her mouth, and the other ripped it away with his teeth. Other grown-ups joined them, dipping their partners low so that their hair washed across the sparkling floor. They spun and groaned in their partners' arms, and their intertwined shadows flickered in the candlelight.

The party went on for hours. Eddie's chair seemed something like a throne, and he held court as the grown-ups drank and drank. He watched the dancing. He watched the flirtations that passed between members of the crowd. He leaned his cheek on his gloved hand and drummed his fingers on his chair and laughed and laughed and then stopped abruptly and then laughed and laughed again.

"This party is fun," he said, "but I think we should do something more."

The grown-ups clapped. "The children!" they cried. "We'll get them up here and tear their hair out."

Luisa tried to stand again, and Andrew yanked her down and gripped her hand more tightly.

Eddie shook his head and yawned. "I'm tired of the children," he said.

"Then what about the man?" the grown-ups cried. "We've already got his eyes, but we could take his hands."

Luisa and Andrew swallowed hard.

"Let's do something new," Eddie said. "Something reckless. Something we've never done before."

The crowd hooted and screamed in anticipation.

Eddie stood up. He raised his scepter high. "I think it's time to hunt a pig."

The clapping stopped, hands arrested almost touching in midair. Red lipsticked mouths hung open. A blonde in a seersucker suit staggered back and caught his weight on the patio's stone wall.

"Follow me," Eddie said. "I'm the only one of you with any imagination. It's why I'm here. You'll love it." He smiled, and his teeth looked like sharpened pearls. He licked his tongue across them. His scepter looked like a spear, and when he stalked down the steps that led to the path, the grown-ups moved behind him, pulling weapons from the folds of their gowns, from the inside breast pockets of their jackets, from the buns on top of their heads. They snapped ropes taut. They held knives up that glittered in the torchlight. Their stiletto heels weren't called stilettos for nothing—they had daggers even on their feet. Somewhere in the background drums started up, and the grown-ups marched down the hill to a kind of pounding furor.

They came so fast that Andrew and Luisa had to jump to get out of their way. A cloud passed over the moon just then, luckily, and the night became temporarily dark. Two of the grown-ups carried torches, but the torches created as many shadows as they did light, and nobody saw the children when they slipped behind another tree.

Luisa and Andrew followed the furious procession, trembling, but moving as quietly as they could, staying in the shadows, hoping the moon would stay behind its cloud until it set. Ahead of them, Eddie separated himself from the rest. He stalked past the hut where Natasha and Mimi and Otis must have been hiding. *Please be asleep*, Luisa thought. She worried that Natasha would wake up and shamble toward the grown-ups, rubbing her eyes and yawning. She always had a hard time staying in bed when she knew people were awake outside. But the hut stayed still, and Luisa muttered thanks to whoever was out there, whoever it was who usually didn't listen.

"Here, piggy piggy," Eddie crooned. The moon, mostly behind clouds, only lit up parts of him. His wrists. His hollow right cheek. His spine, arching like a bow, each ridge casting a shadow that made the rest of his back look striped. "Here, piggy piggy," he crooned, and, out of the dark pen, an answering grunt rose up.

The spotted pig walked out of the shadows and into the torchlight. She moved slowly, like a sleepwalker, without purpose, without will.

"Stop!" Luisa tried to call, but Andrew clapped his hand across her mouth before the words could sound. She tried to bite his palm.

"They're out to kill something," he hissed. "If they don't kill her, they'll kill you."

She fought against him, but not hard enough that he would let her go.

Eddie fanned his fingers in the moonlight. He wore a gold ring over the glove on his right hand, and the torch fire caught on the ring and the ring bent it toward the ground. The pig watched the light as it danced across the earth, the twigs, the fallen leaves that carpeted the pen. Luisa, watching too, thought the light looked like fairy light she'd read about in a book one time, she couldn't remember when. She couldn't take her eyes off it either.

And then, just like that, a story of her own popped into her mind. She was small, much smaller than anyone around her. She held a woman's hand, and stood on a platform, and she was the same level as shopping bags and pocket books and hands in pockets. Everyone was wearing puffy coats, and she was in a puffy coat too, but her coat was unzipped and she couldn't get it zipped back up with just one hand. She tried to pull her other hand free, but the woman said, "Stop wiggling," and held her hand more tightly.

There were stairs just next to them, metal stairs leading down from above, and it seemed the platform filled up constantly with more people climbing down the stairs, that the people arriving would never end. The woman said, "Come on," and pushed forward through the crowd. A track lay down below, a subway track, obviously, Luisa knew as she remembered, but in her memory it wasn't quite so obvious. It was a ditch, a gully, filled with trash and metal rails. She saw a rat run across the pit. She saw another rat, so still that until it flicked its tail, it was invisible. She waited for it to flick its tail, and then she saw a light dance out and skip a circle round the rat.

"Stand still," she heard the woman say. Was it her mother? There was no way this woman was a queen. In her memory, Luisa squirmed but didn't look up. The woman held tight onto her hand.

The light was red. It was just a dot, and sometimes it moved slowly and sometimes it moved quickly. It circled and looped and stuttered. It climbed over Dixie cups and stroked each of the three rails, and explored the walls and even touched her feet. She tried to step back when it skipped across her feet, but the hand held her in place. "Stop moving," the voice above said, and she did. The only thing that moved was her eyes. She couldn't stop watching the red light, but she didn't like it. She didn't like it touching her.

In her memory, they were there on that platform, at the edge of that gully above those tracks, for hours. The train took forever to arrive. The light moved fast and slow. It moved up and down. It came near. It danced away to the far wall. Nothing seemed to stop it, and even the rats eventually ran away. In the distance, when she managed to lift her eyes away from the red dot, she saw a glimmer of white light emerging from the darkness. She squeezed the hand she held.

"It's coming," she heard in reply.

She looked around at the platform then. A man stood next to them. He held something in his hand. It was shaped like a pen, with a rounded end instead of a point. His thumb was on a button, and he clicked the button once. The red light emerged on the floor. He clicked it a second time, and it disappeared. She turned her head to look at him, and he was staring at her and laughing. He turned his light on again, and drew circles on her knees, on her shins, on the tops of her shoes. Then he flicked it off, and the train came, and she and the woman squeezed through the doors and rode away somewhere. She couldn't remember where. She just remembered her face going red, and the heat and crowd of the train, and the feeling that she'd been captured by that light, and how much that man had enjoyed capturing her, and how awful it felt to be caught even without being touched.

She shook her head, torn between a kind of joy in at last remembering something, and a kind of sorrow in wishing it was something else that she'd remembered. She tried to take her eyes off the light from Eddie's ring, but it captured her just as surely as that red light had long ago.

It captured the spotted pig as well.

The pig sunk her snout into the light. She nosed it and chased it and snapped her jaws at it and turned circles while Eddie made it dance. Eddie laughed, and the grown-ups, huddled safely behind him, laughed too, and came nearer, and wiped their drooling mouths with the backs of their hands.

"You're so clever," they cried.

"It's nothing but a silly pig," they cried.

"My spear is sharp," they cried. "Let me go first."

It was harder to see when they moved forward. They carried their torches in front of them, and they gathered in a mass, their bodies blocking the light.

Luisa tried to get to the pig. She tried to stop the chanting crowd. Andrew pulled her back. In the strange light from the torches, the grown-ups' bodies blended together. But then one raised a torch-bearing arm high above their heads, and the light spread out over the spotted pig. The pig moved as if into a spotlight. Another arm raised a spear as high as the torch. The arm fell. The torch stayed high. The pig collapsed, the spear stabbed deep into her belly. She squealed. The mass of grown-ups sighed. The pig kicked her legs, blood ran onto the earth, and in the flickering light the blood looked just like another shadow.

Luisa's shoulders shook. Andrew's arm wrapped around her and kept her from running toward the grown-ups. The hunters, their spears shook, too. Luisa leaned her head against Andrew's cheek, and his cheek was wet with tears.

Below them, the grown-ups were cheering. They'd stabbed the pig a few more times, and now they tied its legs around a spear, pulled it from the pen, and hoisted it onto their shoulders. The brunette in the red dress stood at one end. The man in the white tuxedo stood at the other. Blood dripped and stained the white fabric of his jacket with dark splotches, but it blended right in with the red velvet gown. The pig's mouth was slack. Its eyes were shut. It was heavy, but the two grown-ups seemed up to the task. They carried her in triumph, for once without complaining.

And, oddly, the other pigs stayed sleeping.

The grown-ups marched the pig up the path, right past Andrew and Luisa. The torches came first, and then Eddie, and then the pig bearers, and then the last of the straggling grown-ups. Most were silent, solemn for the first time that the children had ever seen. But the last ones, the ones walking more slowly and so walking in the dark, whispered about bacon and how long it takes to cure.

"Do you think there will be enough chops for all of us?" one said.

"I think so," the other said.

"And what about the tenderloin? I love pork tenderloin."

"As long as none of us is a pig," the other said. They giggled, like children, and smacked their lips.

At first Otis thought the loud sounds outside were the regular nighttime sounds of the island. His ears were sharper than he'd ever realized. But the sounds were too regular to be made by nature, and pretty soon he heard voices chanting, and then soon after that he heard the chanting voices getting close.

"What is that?" Mimi whispered. He hadn't realized she was awake.

"I don't know," he said. "It's voices, but I can't hear what they're saying."

"They're coming from up the hill," she said. He heard her scoot her body across the floor. She settled in against the wall beside him, not touching him, but close. "What do you think they want?" she said.

"I don't know," he said again. "Let's just stay quiet and listen."

She must have nodded, because she didn't answer with her voice.

He wondered if she was scared. He was scared. He didn't mind admitting it. He'd rather not be scared, but not because there was shame in it. He'd rather not be scared because he'd rather there wasn't anything to be scared about. God, there was a lot to be scared about. The world was terrifying. He put his hand out. He held his breath. He felt her small hand slip inside his larger one. He squeezed her hand once, and then held it tight, but not too tight. Had she really come to him for comfort?

"Do you think Andrew and Luisa are okay?" Mimi whispered. "They've been gone a really long time."

"I'm sure they're fine," Otis said. He was lying. Some lies are justifiable, no matter what ethicists say. "They'll get back soon. I'm certain they'll get back."

The crowd seemed to have rushed entirely past the hut now. The drums stilled, and an odd silence descended on the island. Silence, and then the interested grunting of a pig. Then a small fit of giggling. Then a scream. And then the crowd turned and swelled around the hut again, slower now, talking about pork chops, carrying a heavy weight.

Otis kept his arm around Mimi's shoulders and for the first time thought it strange that Natasha was still asleep. He held Mimi against his chest and stroked her hair until she fell asleep, too. His heart rose, just slightly, to realize that, broken or not, he was still capable of comforting a child. He listened to the sounds in the air around him and thought he heard Natasha, sleeping, lick her lips.

The pigs woke up slowly in the morning. They opened their eyes, squinted at the light, and then shut them again. When they finally stood up, they shuffled in a daze around their pen as they'd done every day for a million years, vaguely hungry, vaguely wondering what the world would send to them that day, still halfway in their dreams. It took the mineral smell of blood on leaves for them to realize that one of them was gone.

They were new to crying. They snuffled and shuffled and grunted and moaned and let out short hiccupy sighs and paced back and forth and then breathed in sharply again. They knew nothing about expressing grief. They banged their giant bodies against the fence. They shrunk into themselves. They collapsed on top of one another and tried to turn their five enormous bodies into one. Then they each stood up and stumbled dizzily in opposite directions and cowered alone, not caring if the sun burned their skin bright red. They cried until there was no liquid left to cry. They cried until their ribs were sore from heaving. Their hooves hurt. Their heads hurt. They cried without any hope of comfort.

U p above, the celebration lasted for hours. The spotted pig was gutted and cleaned. A great fire was built and allowed to burn down to glowing coals. Two stands were erected to hold a spit. The coals below the stand glowed red. The pig was speared snout to tail. It roasted slowly all night long, the grown-ups turning it every hour. During the first several hours music was played, fruity drinks were drunk, shoes were removed, and the limbo was danced in a circle around the fire. One grown-up even walked, barefoot, across the coals. As the night wore on, though, and the velvet dark of midnight slipped closer to the milky light of dawn, they tired out and many fell asleep in lawn chairs.

It was hard work turning the spit. It took a lot of muscle. More than once the suggestion was made to wake the children and get them to do the turning, but nobody felt like walking down the path alone in the dark.

Luisa and Andrew themselves fell asleep more than once, crouched down where they hid behind a bush. They nodded off and then shook themselves awake, then nodded off again. They each lost their sense of the other's body, and more than once discovered that in their sleep they'd used the other's back as a pillow, waking up with the imprint of spine on their cheeks and the imprint of grass on their knees. More than once when they woke, they woke whispering that they had to save the pigs, and then they remembered that they hadn't saved the pigs, and then they watched the grown-ups turn the spit, and then they nodded off again. The night seemed to last forever.

It took more than a night to roast a pig, especially one of those pigs. The pigs moved gracefully, but they were enormous, big enough to swallow the world whole. There, on the spit, in the early morning light, the spotted pig, now with its spots burned off, looked like it was frozen mid-stride. Its hind legs were stretched and knotted up behind it. Its forelegs reached out ahead. The bands that cinched its waist to the spit made it look svelte, as if it had lost weight and was dressing for its new body. Its spots were replaced by a flame-kissed orange-gold.

When morning insisted on turning into day, and the sun insisted on shining right into the faces of those asleep on lawn chairs, the grown-ups woke in their soiled party clothes, hung over, backs aching, heads throbbing, aware, suddenly, of what they had done.

"I don't even like pork," one said.

"I'm starving," another said. "But that thing's not going to be done for hours."

"Somebody needs to take over," the one stuck at the spit said. "I've been turning this thing all night."

"Not me," the first one said. "I'm going in to take a shower."

Luisa and Andrew heard the pigs wake up below at the bottom of the hill, and they thought they heard them crying.

The worst thing, though—or maybe not the worst thing, but certainly unfortunate—was that the roasting pig smelled so delicious that Luisa and Andrews' mouths watered uncontrollably, and they felt just like slobbering grown-ups, and they were so tired. So, so tired. They fell asleep again under the bush, their mouths slightly open, drooling even in their sleep.

The world down by the hut was in overwhelming disrepair. Garbage washed ashore in a constant flood, and Mimi carried as much of it as she could to the pigs, but all the pigs would do was nose at it and push it aside and let it pile up in smelly heaps while they lay down right in the hot sun and howled. Their skin was burned almost as crisp as the spotted one's burning on the spit, and they didn't care. They didn't even attempt to look for shade. The day was hot, every day was hot, and before too long flies gathered on the rotting garbage, and then moved from the garbage to the pigs, and the pigs did nothing. They just lay there and let the flies buzz around their eyes.

Finally, thank God, clouds covered up the sun, because Mimi had just realized that the garbage was massing higher than it ever had before, and that it was threatening to form mountains where the water shrugged it onto land, and that the pigs really were turning dangerously pink, and that the next thing she'd have to do was climb right over the fence and into the pen to try to nudge them into the shade. And getting in the pen with the pigs, flattened by grief or not, was not a comfortable thought.

"Eat something," Mimi said to them. They shut their eyes and looked away. "You'll like the first amendment," she said. "How about some rusty nails? Or maybe an old PalmPilot?" They didn't seem interested in the garbage at all.

"Are you sure you don't want to just try my fingernail?" Mimi said. She leaned over the fence and wiggled her fingers. "Try me. I'm here for you." The one with the dainty hooves pushed her face farther into the dirt.

Natasha picked up walnuts and lobbed them over the fence, occasionally hitting the pigs squarely on the snout.

The pigs looked at her, blinked their eyes, and then looked away.

It didn't help that the smell of roasting pig drifted down the hill from above and perfumed the rotten air all day. Mimi's stomach growled. She couldn't help closing her eyes and breathing in the warm, rich odor, tinged just around the edges with the sweetness of apple. Mimi had always claimed she was a vegetarian, but she would have gobbled up a heaping plate of the spotted pig if it were served to her just then, even with the mourning pigs in front of her, even with the sounds of the grown-ups on the path last night still ringing in her ears. It smelled so good. Natasha got a fork out, and tried to climb the fence, tilting her body over it menacingly and calling, "Breakfast!" Only Otis, sitting by the hut, his empty eyes like caverns, seemed unmoved by the smell.

By mid-morning, Mimi got the pig with the lopped-off ear to take a bite of a plastic water bottle. There was never a shortage of anything plastic, and normally any of the pigs would have loved it, but today it took hand feeding to get her to show an interest. Mimi held the bottle by its neck, and if she leaned over far enough, she could get it almost to the pig's mouth. She held it and whistled, and the pig raised her head and sighed.

"Just take a little bite," Mimi said.

The pig looked away.

"For me? Just a little one?"

The pig sniffed the bottle. She looked away again.

"You'll like it," Mimi said. "It's chewy. Remember?"

The pig opened her mouth just a little bit. She stuck out the edge of her tongue and licked the plastic.

"That's right," Mimi said. "It's good."

When the pig snapped down on the bottle, she did it so quickly and with so much force that it was blind luck she didn't take off Mimi's entire hand. As it was, she got just the tip of her pointer, just the nail, really. Just what Mimi had offered her before. There was a little blood, but nothing terrible. And the pig was eating. Pretty soon the other pigs were eating too. Mimi didn't even stop to wrap her finger in her skirt. She just heaved more garbage into the pen and watched the mourning pigs have at it. She hoped that five were enough to do the job six pigs were meant to do.

Where was Otis during all of this? He tried to help. He shuffled down to the water and lifted up handfuls of trash and carried them back to the pigs. But he was not particularly effective, and, to be honest, it was more work to run over and head him in the right direction than it was for Mimi to just do the work herself. She told him to go back and sit down. Maybe she told him a little too forcefully. She couldn't read his expression when he walked away.

And where were Andrew and Luisa? Mimi thought about the drums the night before, the marching feet, the screams. She thought about the pigs in mourning, the despair as strong a stench in the air as the moldering garbage. She needed them home so they could help her. She needed them so she wouldn't have to face all of this alone. Where were they?

It was all hangovers and parties for the grown-ups that day. They lurched into their beds, and went back to sleep, and then they got up and drank gin and tonics, and then lurched to bed again, and then woke up and drank some more. They changed clothes occasionally, and interrupted their drinking and sleeping and dancing to drink espresso, and a few of them redid their hair. Most of all they waited for dinner, hardly keeping the drool that pooled inside their mouths from spilling out.

When it was ready, they ate like savages. They sliced large slabs of roasted pig and piled them high on a platter. Juice dripped down their chins and stained their clothes. Their plates were silver and their napkins linen, but they reached greedily across the table and grabbed whole handfuls and shoved them in their mouths until they could barely chew. When they were done, they unbuckled their belts and pushed their chairs back and collapsed on the grass and moaned.

Otis listened to the pigs crying, and he used his fingers to count what he'd lost. His vision. His wife. His son. His belief that it was possible to protect the good in the world. His ability to make a difference. There was more. His motivation to get off the island. His motivation to get home. He didn't really want to get home anymore. He couldn't explain it, even to himself. He wanted to put his arms around his son. He thought if he could just put his arms around the kid, hug him close to his chest, hold him so he couldn't get away and just keep holding him and holding him, the hollow inside him might fill a little. But he didn't want to pin his child down like that. When he thought about it, it sounded too much like he wanted to put his son in a trap. Who'd have thought that he'd ever think about his own arms as a trap? What else had he lost? His ability to watch a movie. His ability to appreciate the surfaces of a woman's body from afar. His ability to take an interest in the aesthetic properties of architecture.

Garbage was piling everywhere. The five pigs couldn't handle it all. They were so knocked over by their grief that they weren't hungry, and then, beyond that, it had been a perfect system: the world needed six giant stomachs, not five, to consume its trash. When Otis walked down from the hut to the pen to check on them, he twisted his ankle on a broken dot matrix printer. The air smelled like rotting banana peels. The pigs were barely interested in the story of how he lost his virginity, and they didn't bat an eye (or he didn't think they did—he couldn't see—at any rate they didn't change their behavior in the slightest) when he told them about the first time he'd had his heart broken, really broken, crushed to smithereens. He had a horrible moment of thinking that some of his stories, ones that he'd kept close to his heart for more years than he could easily count, might not be so interesting after all.

"We should leave," he called out over his shoulder, trying to aim his voice where he thought Mimi was standing. "This is not something to wait and see about."

"I'll handle it, Otis," he heard Mimi say. He thought about the two of them last night, on the floor of the hut together, her young body against his broken one, his arm around her to help her feel safe. Why was she talking to him like this?

"I'm serious," he called. "We've got to go."

"There's nowhere to go," Mimi said. "We don't have any place left to hide. Besides, the pigs need us. You know that. They can't take care of themselves."

The kid was right. Otis reached his hand over the pen and felt warm ears under his fingers. Their shape was kind of pointy. They probably belonged to the one with dainty hooves. Or maybe the one who was smaller and quicker than the rest. The pig beneath his hand sighed and pushed her head lower into the dirt. Poor thing. So sad. They attacked everyone else. Why hadn't they eaten him? Otis took his hand away and crouched down himself and gathered an armful of garbage. He stood and tipped it over the fence and waited to hear what would happen. Nothing. Just a sad, awful refusal to move. He sighed and turned away.

There had to be someplace they could go. The kids talked about a cave they'd had before Eddie arrived. There had to be more than one cave on the island. And maybe there was even something better than a cave. Maybe there was a place to build another hut deep in the wild center of the place. They could take the pigs with them. They wouldn't be close to the ocean, so the pigs would have to forage for their food, but pigs lived in the wild on countless desert islands; there had to be food for them to eat. Roots. Berries. That sort of thing. From what he'd heard, the pigs had been in their pen forever, eating the world's garbage, growing bigger and bigger to adjust for the world's bloating waste. Why not give them a change of scenery? Why not give them the option to eat what they wanted instead of what the world insisted it could no longer use? He'd never hurt them. The kids would never hurt them. He'd find a place for everyone. Maybe this was why he was here. He'd lead everyone to safety. Let the world solve its own problems.

Otis walked away from the pen. He'd lost track of Mimi. She might be watching him. She might be completely unaware of him. He had no way to know. He tried to walk as casually as possible. He got to the hut and leaned against the wall. Inside he could hear Natasha muttering something about getting her nails done. He walked past the hut. He got to the place where the path forked left to the villa and right to who knew where. He paused. He listened. He heard nothing but insect-filled silence and the soft back-and-forth of the sea. He took a deep breath, chose the path to the right, and started walking.

It didn't take long for the path to become completely overgrown. Before he knew it, he was pushing thorny stalks away from his face. The air was hot and he could feel the sun beating down on his head and he could hear bees throbbing loud in the tangled world around him. The path, or anyway the slight indent in the ground that he followed through the brambles, moved uphill. He sort of liked the idea of moving away from the water. All it brought was trash. Like him. He laughed. It felt good to be moving.

He wandered like that for a long time, feeling terrible about himself, feeling terrible about the world, feeling the sun beat into his skin until it was close to blistering. His bare feet hurt even though their calluses were a quarter inch thick. Eventually the undergrowth opened up to a granite shelf. Otis sat down, pulled his legs up to his chest, and breathed in the clear open air around him. The sun was as intense as it had been before, and the rock beneath him was hot, but he could feel the wideness of the landscape stretching out in front of him. He thought that the hill he had climbed must look gentle from above, thorns and tangles softened out by distance.

He should have brought water. His lips were cracked. He stood up and shuffled off the granite, back to a path, not quite sure if it had any connection to the path he'd come in on, trusting that, by moving upwards, he was moving to the place he wanted.

It happened fast. He stepped on a soft pile of leaves, and then he stepped on air. When he landed hard at the bottom of a pit, he didn't even know how long he'd been falling.

He tested his legs. He didn't think they were broken. He pushed himself up and his wrist made him wince, but he thought at most it was a sprain. He'd broken bones before. It didn't feel like this. He pressed himself against the wall behind him. It was made of dirt, but relatively smooth. The walls must be high enough to throw a shadow over its interior. The shade was some consolation. He raked his hand over the wall behind him, and then stretched his arm to see if he could reach the top. He couldn't. He stood on his toes and reached again. Just earthen wall beneath his fingers, no leveling off to the path above.

It felt subterranean in there even though he could tell by the noises that there was no covering above him. The air smelled like dirt. It felt very still, no breeze anywhere. He thought he might take a rest. He dropped to the ground and propped his back against the earthen wall and just breathed slowly in and out. What was he doing here? What was he thinking, trekking on his own to find a new place to live? It was a misguided effort. The children wouldn't leave their home. Nobody leaves their home until the danger that it places them in is unmistakable, and even then they don't want to leave. Except him. He'd always wanted to leave his home. Now he'd give anything to go back.

Really.

He couldn't think of anything he wanted more than to be sitting at the dinner table eating spaghetti, laughing with Alice when their son slurped a noodle up from his plate and into his mouth, his lips pursed like he was whistling. He couldn't think of anything he wanted more than to shift his eyes, just for a second, to Alice's face, and have her shift her eyes, just for a second, to meet his, and to share between them what it meant to look at their son. He just wanted that small thing. That moment at a table together. That moment of eyes meeting eyes.

But you can't have that, he thought. *Your eyes are gone. You survived a wreck, but you can't go back home on the other side of it.*

He reached for his locket, but it wasn't there. He turned his head and pressed his cheek against the wall. The dirt was cool. A fly—or maybe it wasn't a fly, maybe it was some other kind of insect that hadn't entered yet into his imagination—brushed for just a moment against his arm, then against his shoulder, and then flew, buzzing, away.

So much silence. So much noise. The natural sounds of the island seemed amplified in the pit. Now that he'd noticed the fly, he thought there must be at least ten different kinds of buzzing in the air around him. And leaves brushing against each other somewhere above. And birds calling, God, so many birds. This was something special. He'd never really used his ears before. He could hear things, the differences between things, in ways he hadn't known existed. There was one bird that peeped over and over and over. That's all she did. And one bird that repeated a tune, but with maybe five variations, until another bird answered with a variation that matched but didn't repeat any of the variations that came before. And the dove. Of course the dove. Sometimes he thought he'd strangle that dove if he could ever get his hands on her.

And there was another noise, too, closer. A sort of sniffling, and if he wasn't mistaken, it came from down in the pit not too far from where he was. It almost sounded like a person crying. Which was crazy because he could tell, or thought he could tell, from the way the air felt that there was no other person nearby. Maybe he wasn't as good at this as he thought. The sniffling sounded like crying, where you suck in your breath to try to stop the tears and then have to breathe out and then in again in a wet gulp. He froze and listened hard, and then he felt it: a solid presence close by, warm and smelling of flesh. What was he, a man-eating giant? Flesh? Really? It smelled of human skin. And when he stood up and trailed his hand along the wall, circling toward the presence along the edge of the pit, it shuffled away in front of him.

"Who's there?" he said. "Who are you?"

"Stay away from me," he heard. "You're disgusting. Don't touch me. Stay on the other side."

It was a thin voice, and it sounded familiar. If he could give it a color he'd say light green, like the inside of a sucker on a tree, bendy, fibrous, not quite sure of what it could do. He thought it was ridiculous to think of a voice like this, but he couldn't help it. It was like the birds: without his sight, voices emerged as being more textured than he'd ever thought of them before. He knew who it was. It was that kid. Eddie.

He'd been there when they'd taken his eyes. He remembered the boy's hands holding him down. They'd looked like they'd never done an hour of work in their lives. Funny that he had noticed that. You'd think he would have been so caught up in being scared that he wouldn't have noticed anything about the world, but he was finding that, even in the deepest pit of despair, it was harder not to notice than to notice. He wondered if everyone turned into a philosopher when they lost their vision or if it was just him.

"You're Eddie, right?"

The sniffling stopped. He'd been right—it *was* the kid he was picturing. Or maybe not picturing. Maybe sensing. Or just simply remembering. Remembering didn't necessarily imply vision. Maybe that's the word he should stick with from now on, strike picture from his vocabulary.

"What are you doing here?" Otis said.

"I fell in," came the answer.

"How could you fall in? Didn't you see it?"

"I wasn't looking. I was thinking about the pigs, okay? I was trying to figure out if it helped to kill one, if it made me feel any better, and I wasn't paying attention. I hurt my ankle."

Beyond his sulky voice, the kid sounded scared.

"Did it help?" Otis asked.

"No," Eddie said. "It didn't help at all."

There was silence for a little while. Otis wanted to tell Eddie that he'd done terrible things a million times to try to make himself feel better. He wanted to tell Eddie that it didn't necessarily make him a bad person. But he couldn't say it. If doing terrible things didn't make you a bad person, what did?

"Can you walk?" Otis finally said.

"Barely."

"How big is this pit?"

"Not that big. Maybe ten feet by ten feet. With ten foot walls."

"It sounds like a trap. Is it a trap? Did your friends build it as a kind of hunting strategy?"

"I don't know," Eddie said. "I guess it is a kind of trap. This is the first I've seen of it. My guess is this island has a lot of hidden places that no one bothers to talk about."

Otis sat down with his back against a dirt wall. He traced his hand across the ground and crumbled dirt between his fingers.

"Are you sure you can't walk?" he said.

"Maybe I can hobble a little," Eddie said. "But it hurts when I put my weight on it."

Otis shook his head. Everyone was so afraid of pain.

The dove warbled in the forest.

"Listen," Otis said. "If I crouch down and you climb on my back, do you think you would be high enough to hoist yourself over the edge?"

There was silence. He wondered why it was taking Eddie so long to answer.

"I think so," he finally heard. "It will be a stretch, but I'm taller than I used to be. Let's do it fast. I'm late for dinner. I thought of something else that might help me feel better."

"Okay," Otis said. "I'll kneel down. Step onto my back. Pull yourself up. Then reach down and help me after you."

He knelt. He put his hands on the pit's earthen floor, and pressed his head between them. He flattened his back as much as he could. He tried to think of himself as a table. Or a park bench. Or even a birdbath without water. He waited for Eddie to climb onto him, and the waiting was almost as heavy as Eddie was when he finally took his first step.

It was like he was made of solid bronze. Otis thought his spine would splinter. The air drained out of his lungs. He gasped. The other foot landed on top of him as well, and he was certain he would be crushed, left flat in a grave ten times too big for his body. He wanted to call out, but the air that left his lungs pulled any words he had along with it, and the only sound that came out of him beyond the gasping was a kind of dry heaving and shaking of his body around emptiness.

And then Eddie pressed into him one time harder, if harder was even possible, and then he let out a long pork-smelling burp, and then he was gone. Otis heard a scrabbling above him, a grunting, and then quiet.

It took him too long to get his breath back. By the time he could manage words, the silence up above was so strong that he knew before he even asked that Eddie had left without helping him. He wasn't surprised. Well, a little surprised. But it didn't change the way he thought about the world. He would have done the same thing ten years ago, twenty years ago. Who was he kidding—he did the same thing every time he shipped out to sea. He was good at leaving problems behind. And that's what he was now, on this island, maybe everywhere in his life. A problem. A middle-aged man who wanted to do good but who caused trouble whenever he tried. Who was he kidding? He wasn't even quite inside middle age anymore. He was heading past it, toward whatever stage comes next. He didn't know the name for it. Not old man exactly. Something in between the middle and the end.

He stood up. He pressed his hands against the wall. He shuffled to his left, feeling up and down on the crumbling surface, smelling warm dirt around him, wondering when the heat of day would turn to the cool of night. He thought that if he had found his way into a children's book, his fingers, sensitized through his lack of sight, would find the outline of a little door, and that he would pry that door open and set out exploring the world beneath the hillside. His lack of sight would actually be an advantage because in the dark world below the hill, creatures would have to navigate by sound. But this wasn't a children's book despite its setpiece similarities—Otis was pressed tight in his own life, as odd as that life had turned out to be. There was no door. There was only rough wall and, suddenly, a rope.

And a voice at the top of the pit saying, "Use the rope. I'll help you up."

It was Mimi.

"What the hell is this pit?" he said.

"I don't know," she said. "But I figured out how to braid reeds into twine."

"Eddie said he'd help me, but then he left."

"I'm not surprised," Mimi said. "You can't trust him. I tied the rope to a tree. See if you can hold onto it and walk your feet up the wall. I think maybe it sounds harder than it actually is."

"Okay," Otis said, and grasped the rope. His body went horizontal and stayed horizontal while he walked his feet up. And then his feet were on a flat surface instead of a wall, and Mimi's hands were pulling him beneath his arm-pits. Then his body was lying splayed out on the path. He thought how glad he was not to be breathing in the smell of earth anymore, how glad he was not to be buried alive.

"Don't step backward," Mimi said. "The pit's still there even if you can't see it. I'll take you back to the hut."

"I don't want to go back to the hut," Otis said.

"Well that's ungrateful," Mimi said.

And there she was: Alice. He could spend his whole life atoning for the way he'd treated her.

"Don't talk to me like that," Otis said.

"How am I supposed to talk to you?"

"With respect."

"Do something that's worth respect and I'll talk to you with respect."

It was uncanny the way Mimi's vocal rhythms mimicked Alice's exactly. Even her tone shifted to Alice's alto pitch.

"All you do is run," he heard. "You run and run and run and never look back and you have no idea at all that every-thing you're running from is exactly the same as everything you're running toward. You broke my heart? You broke your son's heart? You have your own broken heart ahead. In fact, it's probably not even ahead. You're probably running with a broken heart right now and the reason you can't go fast enough is because you're broken and you just don't work."

He gasped. He thought he couldn't feel anything worse than having his eyes ripped out, but having his wife conjured from nothing, having her here and having her say what she said, he felt crushed to the ground, crushed below the ground, crushed into dust and then ground into the ground.

"Okay," he said. "I'll come back with you. I won't run away again."

"Okay," Mimi said. "Glad to hear it."

As soon as night fell, the party started up again. Torch-es flickered, and men and women shrieked in fren-zy. They ate until they reached bone, and then gnawed on bones until the carcass fell apart. Luisa and Andrew woke up cramped and shivering under a bush, disoriented at first, and then hungry.

Even though they ate and ate like animals, the grown-ups stayed hungry, too.

"We need more," the grown-ups cried. "We'll never be full."

Their hands and their arms and their chins and their clothes dripped with grease. Their feet and their legs and their elbows and their shoulders glowed where sparks from the embers of the roasting fire leapt to fleck their skin. They shredded pork and gulped wine and belched long, protract-ed burps. Their sequined dresses, their starched white shirts, their elbow-length gloves were oily and torn.

Eddie stood at the head of the table. He alone moved with a kind of grace although, if Luisa and Andrew looked carefully, he did seem to be favoring one ankle. He looked out at the gathered crowd, at the distended bellies, at the bodies slumped over plates. They were so stuffed, those grown-ups, that they could barely lift their heads to look at him. The redhead reached a hand out to touch his arm, but got distracted along the way and grabbed a wineglass instead and lifted it to her mouth and drank wine as if it were juice.

"I'm full, but I'm still hungry," Eddie said. There was a little blood, or maybe wine, at the corner of his mouth.

"I'm tired of pork," he cried. "I'm tired of cakes. I want something more tender."

"More tender," the grown-ups echoed. They nodded their heads like they knew what he was talking about, but most of them were too busy eating to pay much attention.

"I want something young," he said. "I want something that's hardly been weaned off milk."

"Something young," they cried. Or some of them did. Maybe one. A brunette whose lipstick was smeared across her face and who had grease smudges on her cheeks. The redhead smacked the brunette with the back of her hand, but she was close to passing out, and when the smack landed it was more like a pat. "What you want is a baby something," she said, but without a whole lot of interest. "Maybe a baby pig. A piglet—a suckling pig. I don't think we have any here, though. Our pigs are old." She popped another piece of pork in her mouth, but she was so full that she opened her mouth almost immediately and let the half-chewed meat fall, gummy, on her plate.

"I don't want a piglet," Eddie yelled. "I want a child. A child roasted on a spit. It doesn't matter if we're still waiting for the next lot. I want one now." He glared out at the rest of them, waiting for a reaction, and one by one they opened their eyes. A man with a bow tie coughed. A woman with a rose in her hair sat up straight. The brunette with the smeared lipstick threw her napkin over her plate and stood up and clapped. The redhead followed her lead, rousing herself to wobble up to standing, and the rest did, too, clapping slowly at first and then so fast and so loud that it sounded as though the sky was caving in.

Eddie watched them, smiling, and then climbed on top of the table, his arms raised high. He paced across it from end to end, his gold sandaled feet stepping between plates, over platters, around overturned goblets and pitchers of wine. "We have four of them down below," he said. "Four of them, and they're not doing their jobs. I can smell the garbage all the way up here. If they're not working, what good are they? Think of them trussed and tender. Think of them laid out on plates." The fire glowed at the roasting pit. Eddie's teeth looked sharp.

Andrew and Luisa, watching from the shadows, gulped.

"We've got to do something," Luisa said.

"I know," Andrew said. "I think it's really time to hide."

"No," Luisa said. "We've got to stop him. We can't keep running forever. It's an island. There aren't that many places to go."

"But what can we do?" Andrew said. "He's practically got an army surrounding him."

"It's now or never," Luisa said. "Things are getting worse. Next time they hunt us, they're going to cook us up."

"That's disgusting," Andrew said.

"I know," Luisa said. "But look at them. They're not worried about being disgusting."

The remains of pig gristle stuck to the sides of the grownups' faces. Globs of fat glistened through their hair. Elegant up-dos were half-fallen and covered in grease. Hands, heavy with rings, clutched at the tablecloth. Eddie, striding among them, nudged their faces with his foot. They clapped. They screamed. They salivated. They drooled.

"Let's take him," Luisa said.

"What?" Andrew said.

"Now. Grab him. Let's hold him hostage until they say they'll leave us alone."

"That's crazy," Andrew said. "I'm not going near him. He looks like he could bite. Plus, he's got all those people there to stop us."

"They're drunk," Luisa said. "And they're loud, but they're not organized. Most of them were asleep five minutes ago. They ate so much they probably won't be able to move for days."

Eddie had climbed down now and started beating the table with his scepter. Each time the scepter fell, the table shook and the grown-ups shuddered. "Sit up," he cried. "Sit up straight. I'm talking. Listen to me." It was hard to imagine that the grown-ups would listen to him. He was in such a frenzy that he stabbed one or two hands with the sharp point of the scepter, and his nudging sometimes turned into hard kicks. But the grown-ups just clapped and clapped and clapped despite their bleeding hands. "Wake up, wake up, wake up," he called. They were sleepy, and struggling to stay awake, and even though their clapping was loud, their motions seemed still thick with slumber.

"Okay," Andrew said. "You're right. What should we do?"

Luisa led the way. Amazingly (and she was amazed at it, too), she didn't trip. They crept up behind Eddie where he pounded at the head of the table. On their way they picked up the greasy rope that had been used to truss the pig. Andrew snatched a linen napkin. Luisa grabbed a shank bone, stripped of meat and glistening white.

It was easy to approach unheard. Eddie was pounding the table, gulping down glasses of wine, and then pounding the table again. The grown-ups yelled and clapped, but they didn't look at the world closely. If anything, the furor made it impossible for them to focus. One of them might have seen them, but when she raised her voice and pointed, it blended in with all the other sounds. Most of them used the spaces between claps to rub their eyes.

Luisa looked at Andrew and nodded. Andrew nodded back. Luisa raised the shank high. Its balled end caught the light. It looked even sturdier than Eddie's scepter. She waited for Eddie to bend down to pick up a plate. Then, using all her body's strength, she slammed the bone down on Eddie's head.

It worked.

Eddie collapsed on the ground behind the table. The grown-ups looked about, bewildered and laughing and, uncertainly, they kept on clapping. Eddie lay motionless on the ground, like a child there, sleeping through his pain.

Andrew shoved the napkin in his mouth and knotted the ends behind his head. Luisa used the rope to tie his hands behind his back. The rope was long enough that she could cut it in two and she used the second half to tie Eddie's ankles together as well. They pulled Eddie up, and Andrew put his hands under his armpits, and Luisa grabbed his feet. His toenails were sharp, and his legs were heavy, and his cologne made them both gag, but they carried him. And with each step they took farther away from the table and the fire, his weight became more manageable.

Was it their imagination, or did his body take on a more familiar, human quality as they dragged him down the path? Eddie's arms at first had felt like solid gold, but now they were clearly flesh. They could poke it and see the blood rush up around the indent that their fingers made. His toenails at first had been as sharp as razors, but though Luisa's arms bled where they'd sliced her, they now looked like they were just ordinary nails in need of a trim. He was heavy, and unwieldy, but the more they looked at him, the more he looked like a boy—a boy with a sulky mouth and doughy skin and hair that had been dyed an odd shade of blonde, and that maybe wore too much makeup, but human.

Still, it was a passed-out body they were carrying, and he was heavy. It took them a long time to get back to the hut, and they were exhausted by the time they got there. Dawn had just spread her fingers across the water when they dragged Eddie's body to the threshold. A rosy light spread out over the hut and the pen and the frothy water that edged the coast. The air smelled awful, of rotting cabbage and rotting fish and coffee grounds and hard boiled eggs and something chemical that was impossible to place. There were mounds of refuse on the grass and mounds of refuse at the water and the mounds clogged the path to the pen so thickly that it was hard to even know where the path was underneath it all.

They were just about to open the door when it opened on its own. Otis stepped out, Mimi's arm through the crook of his elbow as guide, his face a series of hollows. From behind them, a girl's voice recited lists of dresses she would some-day own: ball gown, sundress, a-line, shift. Eddie groaned. Luisa kicked him. Just inside the pen, a pig lay with her legs outstretched, so vulnerable in the morning light that there wasn't anything to do but cry.

"We've got to run," Luisa said. "Now."

Otis and Mimi nodded. Everyone agreed it was finally time to go.

From a distance, when the wind was just right, the smell of garbage crept along the edge of the entire world. From a distance, everyone said they prayed the island would remain in place forever, but even from a distance, everyone secretly hoped it would sink into the sea.

Mimi tied Otis's hair back, but strands came loose and hung in a greasy, snot-filled veil across his face. He wasn't good at running. He stumbled over everything and after a while he didn't even bat away the flies when they occasionally left their halo formation and landed on his nose.

When Andrew tried to help, Mimi waved him off. Andrew said, "Fine," and got to work on Natasha. "Natasha," he said. "We have to hurry."

"No," she said.

There it was: the voice. Sweet and clear and clean. Each time it sounded, it made the inside of Otis's heart vibrate like he'd been waiting his whole life to hear it without even knowing he was waiting. But "no"? Was that really what he'd been waiting for?

The grown-ups' cries thundered from above.

"Yes," Andrew said. "Now."

"No," she said again.

Was it just Otis's imagination, or did Natasha's voice make the pigs come running? He could hear them now, throwing themselves against the fence, grunting and snorting and landing hard. Had she roused them out of mourning? Were they ready to help?

"Look at the ocean," Andrew said. "Listen to the grownups. Listen to the pigs. We need to hide. We need shelter. It's bad."

Mimi didn't seem to care that Natasha wasn't moving. She was brushing loose hair off Otis's forehead and whispering to him not to cry. He wasn't crying. He'd moved on to something else, but it was like she hadn't noticed, like she couldn't see him. That was ironic. But true. It would be all right, she said, *shh*. Otis moaned and rested his head in her hand.

Luisa was inside, gathering bedrolls. Eddie just lay there, unconscious, with his hands behind his back. His legs seemed to constantly get in the way. Mimi kicked them whenever they found their way toward where she stood. Andrew sighed. He forced Natasha's arms away from her knees, and wrapped them around his neck. "On my back," he said. "I'll carry you. Just don't choke me."

So they ran as best they could.

Luisa carried a sack filled with blankets and food. Mimi held Otis's arm and pulled him along the path. Andrew carried Natasha on his back. They tried to drag Eddie, but he woke up when they pulled him over the first rock. He opened his eyes and for a second looked confused. Only for a second though, and then confusion was replaced by anger. He threatened at first, but after a couple of punches they untied his ankles and he started walking, sulky and annoyed. His bottom lip jutted out. He walked behind Otis so close that from time to time he stepped on Otis's heels. Otis was pretty sure he did it on purpose, but he still remembered that kid and the way he'd laughed when Otis's eyes were gouged, and he found he was reluctant to tell him to walk more carefully.

Eddie felt his sister's hands. They pressed into his arms and gripped his skin the same way he gripped his own skin when he was trying to remember who he was.

The gag inside his mouth tasted of pig and made it almost impossible to breathe. He tried to jerk his arm away, but Luisa held on tight.

She had him. She'd pushed him to the edges of the net. She'd left him behind in the pantry. But now she was collecting him back. If only she'd held onto him when he'd first arrived. If she had, he would never have done what he did. He wished he were a small child again. How had he turned into a killer? How had he gone from being a boy to being whatever it was he'd become?

He had been terrified inside the barrel. It was such an obvious reaction to the situation that he was almost embarrassed to admit it, but, tossing on the waves, enclosed in the dark, the damp and the groaning boards and the weight of the water all around, he'd been so afraid he'd constantly had to work against throwing up. Seasickness hadn't helped, but it had been terror more than anything that made him sick. Now it seemed like terror was the only thing he understood. Kill the children? He could have done it easily. Well, now they had him.

The rope chafed his wrists. He kept his eyes shut and pretended he was asleep and let them push him along the path. His teeth were sharp and when he ran his tongue against them it snagged on their points and his mouth filled up with blood.

His sister had abandoned him two times now. Some people react to betrayal by coiling up inside themselves and never coming out again. Some people react to betrayal by turning wholeheartedly on those who have betrayed. How could he help it if he was the second kind of person? It wasn't his fault. None of this was his fault.

He kicked his foot against a shin as they dragged him along the path, and he let his body go limp, let himself drift like a shipwrecked sailor toward an island's solid shores. And then they untied him. Rescue had come at last.

They ran and ran as if they'd never stop running. Everyone was silent except for Natasha. Now that she could speak, she seemed to have a thousand things to say.

"The lop-eared one's my favorite," she said. "Sometimes we sing each other songs.

"I once watched the skinny one twist in the air three times before she caught a shoe," she said. "She practices. She doesn't think anyone's watching, but she has to work to get up that high. She does it in the shade, when the other pigs are sleeping. She knows I know. That's why she doesn't like me.

"Handbags are my favorite things," she said. "I hate it when we have to throw them to the pigs. And they don't even like handbags. They'd rather eat broken toasters."

She was heavy. Andrew had been working hard for days. He'd discovered Otis with his hollowed eyes. He'd watched a pig get slaughtered and then roasted and then eaten. He'd bound and gagged a boy in front of a sea of grown-ups too frenzied and overfull to notice. Now that he thought about it, he hadn't just been working hard for days; he'd been working hard forever. And now he ran through scrub and brush, skirting a pit, avoiding a giant rock, up hill and down, sun overhead, ocean like diamonds sparkling in the distance, with a chatty toddler on his back who grew heavier by the minute. And if her fluency was any indication, she seemed to be aging as they ran.

"I'd like a new dress," she said. She seemed unaware that her weight might be a burden. "Maybe in pink. I want something with lace at the hem. I want something that bells out when I twirl.

"Can you help me with my homework?" she said. "Long division is tough.

"I think I'm old enough to get a driver's license," she said. "And I think it would really help us all if I had that kind of independence."

Her hands were still tiny. Andrew could feel them at his neck. She had five fingers on each of them. He imagined that her fingernails could use a cleaning, but he couldn't stop to look.

Eddie was stepping on Otis's heels again. Mimi was essentially carrying the man's entire weight. Only Luisa moved with intent. She ran, but she also searched under bushes for hidden entrances to caves. Nothing so far, but she didn't stop trying.

The grown-ups howled in the distance.

They had climbed high now. The ocean was so bright below that the island was ringed by light. They beat a path through scrub. They jabbed their feet on jagged rocks. Bees flushed from lavender in clouds as they pounded by.

"I've never tried an egg cream," Natasha said. "Egg anywhere near soda sounds disgusting, but I've heard they're good."

"There are no eggs in egg creams," Otis said.

"Shh," Mimi said. "You need your rest."

He was nearly doubled over with the effort of running, but he shook his head and panted out the information. Talking seemed to distract him from the pain. "An egg cream is just chocolate syrup and soda water. The origin of its name is a mystery."

"I don't believe you," Natasha said. "Can you make me one?"

"We have to find a cave," Andrew said. "The grown-ups are looking for us. We're not safe. Besides, if we had the ingredients for egg creams, we'd have to give them to the pigs."

"The pigs wouldn't like them," Natasha said. "They don't like anything with carbonation."

"It doesn't matter," Andrew said.

"It does," Natasha said. "You don't believe me, but it does."

Luisa must have found something. She was crouched on the ground in front of some kind of pricker bush. She was pulling canes away, reaching her hand beneath the brush. She crouched lower, her face turned sideways, her right ear near the ground. Then they all heard it—a kind of cooing. She reached in again, and this time pulled something out: the dove. Andrew recognized it immediately. It seemed forever ago that he'd untangled it from thorns beside the sea.

"She had her wing caught," Luisa said. "She was cowering inside there, waiting for someone to help."

"She does that all the time," Andrew said. "I think she gets hurt on purpose. I helped her, too, a while ago. Put her back. We don't have time for her now."

"I'm not going to put her back," Luisa said. He'd never really noticed what she looked like before. She had brown hair. She had skinny legs. Her eyes were brown with just a few flecks of green, and her cheeks were round, and she had a dirt smudge extending from her right ear all the way across her cheek. "She's coming with us," Luisa said.

"I'd love a dress with a feather collar," Natasha said.

Otis groaned.

Mimi remained silent and patted Otis's arm.

"Let's go," Luisa said. She took off running again, slower now with the dove nestled against her chest. They all followed her.

How he knew the grown-ups were still behind them, Otis couldn't say. He heard the children complaining about the brightness of the ocean, the way it practically turned them blind to look at it. He heard them talk about a heaviness inside them, the way they felt soaked through with sadness. He heard war drums in the distance, and the children said there were flares shot up to burst against the sun. Whatever it was that told him, there was no question now that the hunt continued strong.

They passed their old cave with its limestone walls and vaulted door. The jugs of water, the stone ready to plug the hole. Carefully planned, but useless.

They passed a grove of olive trees with thickened, twisted trunks. The light that siphoned through their leaves was silver. The ground that covered their roots was soft.

They passed white rocks grown over with sea fennel and oregano and thyme.

They passed wide swaths of wild grass, feathery and sharp.

The island was filled with unknown places, with unexplored valleys, with hills as high as mountains and rocks as big as ships erupting from the soil. Its folds hid streams and groves and cliffs and gullies, unseen, unknown, passed through quickly now.

They scrambled between boulders. They twisted their ankles. They tore their nails clawing at rock. They followed streams to their source. It was ludicrous that they'd never put in place a backup plan, ludicrous that they hadn't found another cave immediately after they'd lost the first one. It was ludicrous that they didn't know every stone on that island. From a distance, the world might have laughed at them, but it would have stopped laughing when it realized the system that kept the world in balance was broken, too, and it didn't have a backup plan, either.

"Will you take me for a haircut when this is over?" Natasha murmured. She was getting sleepy. "Will you buy me a new nightgown? Will you get me riding lessons?"

"In here," Luisa hissed.

They turned toward her. She was standing on a rock in a stream, pointing at a waterfall. She pulled Mimi and Otis onto the rock beside her, and shoved them through the falling water.

"It's a cave," she said. "A perfect one. I was getting a drink and for a second there the water turned to glass and I could see through it like looking through a window. There's room enough for all of us, and the water will block the noises any of us make. Listen. Otis is probably wailing in there and we can't hear a thing." They all looked pointedly at Eddie. He scowled and turned his eyes toward the ground.

Otis wasn't wailing, actually, and he could hear what she was saying perfectly through the water, but he didn't say anything. He just wanted them safe inside with him.

"Okay," Andrew said. "Let's get inside, quick." He followed Luisa onto the rock. Then he followed Mimi and Otis through the water. He was dripping when he got inside, and Natasha was dripping, too, but it was dry in the cave. The ground wasn't nearly as hard as it looked. Luisa came last, with Eddie and the dove. They all collapsed on the earthen floor. Luisa undid Eddie's gag.

"What should we do now?" he asked. His voice cracked. His hands were still tied behind his back, but with his back against the cave wall and his knees to his chest, he looked almost normal, just a little shinier and with a look on his face like he knew he had no friends.

"Wait," Luisa said. "What else is there to do but wait?"

It was disconcerting for Luisa that Eddie was with them. She looked at him with his back against the wall and she thought about listening to him, just a little while ago, calling for a child to be strung up and roasted over a fire. Just a little while ago he was the one who'd come up with the idea to kill a pig. Just a little while ago he'd pushed her down on her knees in bleach and threatened to pin her hand to the floor like it was a butterfly waiting to be pinned to a page. How could he be with them? Was he their prisoner? He looked so sad. Maybe they had rescued him. Maybe it was more complicated for her because they were related. She felt responsible, somehow, for the awful things he'd done. She picked up pebbles from the cave floor and threw them at him. Her aim was never very good, and it was dark, but she managed to hit him a couple of times.

"Ow," he said. "What are you doing?"

"Hitting you," she said.

"Stop it."

"Why should I?" Luisa said. She lobbed another stone and heard it hit its target.

"Ow," Eddie said again. "Stop throwing rocks at me. Isn't anyone going to stop her?"

Luisa waited to hear if anyone said anything, but Otis was talking to himself, softly, and the rest of them were silent. Who knew, they might have been asleep.

"You got the grown-ups to kill a pig," Luisa said. "You tried to get them to kill us. They're hunting us right this minute because of you."

"I didn't get them to do anything," Eddie said. "They're adults. They make their own decisions."

"I'm your sister," Luisa said.

"That doesn't mean a whole lot to me," Eddie said. "Or at least it didn't. Things are different now, though. I don't feel quite as angry anymore. I mostly feel scared." It sounded true. His voice was small and sad and very exposed.

It must be hard for him to talk honestly, Luisa thought. *It's hard to admit you've made a mistake, to admit you've been horrible, or to come up with an explanation as to why you've been the way you've been.* "How can we trust you?" she said.

"I don't know," Eddie said. "I don't think you'll ever be able to trust me. I think you'll always have to keep your eye on me. I'm just trying to be honest. Don't throw rocks at me anymore. Please don't."

Luisa threw one more rock, then stopped. Most of them had missed anyway. Her brother. She threw rocks at her own feet instead.

They waited through the night, and they waited through the day, and they waited far into the night again. Luisa used some dried leaves to make a nest for the dove, and it huddled in seclusion in the back left corner of the cave. Natasha slept and slept. Eddie said "Sorry," over and over and over until the rest told him to just shut up and go to sleep. Otis said the blackness of night in the cave was the same as the blackness of living sightless in the world, and he said he would be happy in this cave forever. Nobody believed him, but they were glad that he had a positive outlook on things. And at a certain point he started telling stories again.

"When I was first a father," he said, "I couldn't believe how small my child was. He fit exactly in my arms, just his feet dangling out. He gripped my finger from the first time I held him. You don't know what it's like to love until you hold your baby in your arms.

"My wife," he said. "My love for her was nothing compared to the love I felt for that baby. I couldn't tell her, of course, but there was no comparison. A child is a child and wants nothing but love. A spouse is much more complicated. I'm sure she would say the same about me, but we'd never say it to each other.

"I didn't want to leave. I had no choice. The ship was sailing. I had a place on it. There was no way I could have stayed at home. But I cried when I left, and felt no shame in crying."

It was interesting to listen to him talk, but Andrew wanted time alone. The problem with cave-living, he thought, was that you never had any privacy. It was too dangerous to go outside, and there were no rooms separating you from your companions on the inside. The stone walls made everything echo. It gave him a headache. He wanted to go off by himself and just be quiet. He was tired of noise, tired of helping people and listening politely to whatever it was they wanted to say. He wondered what the pigs were up to. He wondered what the island looked like without them there to tend to it.

"You know," Otis said. "Some people would say that dove is a god. Or a goddess. More likely a goddess. We should treat it well. I think I remember a dove flying out of a fire a long time ago.

"You know," he said. "Some people would say we're lucky to be in a cave. Some people would say we should count our blessings instead of dwelling on our problems. Not necessarily me. But some people."

Andrew wondered where the grown-ups were. He wondered whether the waterfall really did drown out sound. He wondered, too, about the matter of supplies. They had plenty of water, being hidden behind a waterfall, but no cup to collect it in. They only had a little food, just some nuts Luisa had grabbed on their way out, and those were mostly gone. They had no way to make a fire, or any way to vent the fire if by some crazy stroke of luck they managed to get one started. They might be safe in the cave right now, but it wasn't viable for the long term. Things had changed since Eddie arrived. Send a child to shore in a barrel, and it throws everything off kilter.

"Sometimes the pigs let me pet them," Mimi said. She was sitting with her back to a wall, across the cave from Andrew. It was odd to hear her talk. She'd seemed so single-minded lately, so taken up with making sure that Otis was okay. "Or anyway, they used to, before they ate my fingers. I was younger then. I thought they loved me. I used to sneak off by myself and stick my hand through the fence and pat them on their heads. I think they liked it."

"I used to do that, too!" Luisa said. She scooted over and leaned her back against the wall right next to Mimi. "Did you have a favorite one? I could never decide, but I thought the skinny one liked me best. I called her Baby, because she was smaller than the others—you know?"

Mimi nodded. "I liked the one with dancer's feet. Lady. That's what I called her."

"Lady. That makes sense. Is she the one that got your fingers?"

Mimi rubbed her hands together and nodded. From where Andrew was sitting, her finger nubs looked just like regular fingers.

"Give me two logs, some twine, and a piece of cloth, and I'll give you a ship that can sail across the ocean," Otis said.

"I'd love a servant," Natasha murmured in a sleepy voice. "Mimi, will you be my servant?"

"I'm pretty sure that when Lady bit them off, she did it as cleanly as she could," Mimi said. "She wouldn't have done that if she didn't love me."

Andrew wished they would all be quiet. He wished he were alone. He wished it had been him who'd thought to name the pigs. He thought he'd known those creatures so well, but maybe he didn't know them at all.

Eddie should have made the difference, as horrible as he was. Three boys now, counting Otis, and three girls. There was balance. Andrew thought he shouldn't have to feel pushed out to the edges anymore. But Eddie just sat there, silent now that he was done saying sorry. He wedged himself into the very back of the cave. The only parts of him that Andrew could see were his golden curls which were fading quickly to light brown. But still, three boys, three girls. Andrew would never be pushed around again.

But had he been pushed around? He tried to remember. Things had been different before Eddie arrived. Life had just moved along, so many surprises that surprises just became part of the normal everyday routine. Single shoelaces. Book reports with whole paragraphs crossed out. Peanut butter granola bars that everybody hated. Used-up batteries. Eight track tapes. Stupid plastic hammers printed from a 3-D printer. You never knew what might show up, what treasure you might find. Then there was the day that Eddie arrived, and the surprise of it: was he there as garbage, and if so, were they all originally there as garbage, and if so, what did it say about their relationship with the pigs? A boy in a barrel. Children on an island enclosed by trash. Things had gotten bad since Eddie landed. Things had been thrown out of balance, and matching three girls with three boys wasn't enough to put it back in order.

We could play tug of war, Andrew thought. *The three of us against the three of them. We'd have to untie Eddie's hands, but it could work. We'd probably win, with Otis's upper body strength and Eddie's willingness to fight dirty and the girls' missing fingers.*

We could do the hunting, and the girls could do the cooking, Andrew thought. *I'm not sure we could trust Eddie with a weapon, but I could supervise him. Otis might not be able to see, but he could build our bows for us.*

We could chop the fire wood, and the girls could knit us sweaters.

He sat in the dark and dreamed up plans, but he knew in the four corners of his mind that as long as the grown-ups were hunting them, it was nuts to plan anything.

He felt a hand slip into his hand. He heard a voice close to his ear. "I'm scared," Luisa said. "I'm too scared to fall asleep."

"I know," he said. "It's bad."

They held hands for a long time. Then they lay down on the cold cave floor and touched their foreheads together and shut their eyes. The waterfall rushed down at the door, and the cave felt damp, and the world was loud. If someone had been able to look down on them from above—if the cave roof had turned to glass, and the starlight had fallen across their bodies, and there was someone up there to look in— that someone would have seen immediately that all six lay in a circle, their heads close together, their hands reaching out in their sleep to hold the hands of their neighbors. But of course there was no one watching. And of course in their sleep they had no way of apprehending their own closeness.

From a distance, word got out that things had changed. The pigs—for whatever reason—were less efficient. Garbage piled up on the world's own home shores. Everyone searched uneasily for a solution. Maybe there was another island somewhere that was filled with hungry pigs? Maybe there was a way to make robotic pigs that did the same thing as real ones? But what island? In what ocean? And how would anyone know how to find it? Just keep dumping the garbage was the policy adopted. Just drop it behind you, move on, and hope that, were you for some crazy reason inclined to look back, it would form a nice neat path right to the open jaws of a herd of reinvigorated pigs, and that five pigs would be enough, and that no one would ever have to take responsibility for mistakes that had been made.

O tis listened to the children sleeping. He listened to the dove turning in circles before tucking her head under her wing and falling asleep as well. He listened to the water tumbling down at the cave's entrance and to the sound of each child's breath as it blew softly from each child's body. He wouldn't sleep that night, he thought. He wasn't sure he'd ever sleep again.

He'd never see his boy again. He'd never see Alice again. He'd never see anything again, not even once, not even if he repented everything he'd ever done in his entire life and begged and begged to be able to start over. There was no chance for starting over. There was only the chance of moving on.

In his mind, he reached his hand out and touched Alice's face. In his mind he told her he was sorry. In his mind he trusted her with their son's future and trusted her with his memory and trusted her to build a life that was better than the one he'd broken each time he'd left her alone on shore.

The children and Otis held a lottery the next day to decide who should venture out to look for food. Andrew and Luisa drew the short sticks. Of course they did. Nobody was surprised.

The dove was becoming a problem. It was hungry, and it shat wherever they wanted to sit, and it wasn't nearly as snuggly as it had first seemed to be. The water thundered louder than its cooing, but even so, the cooing drove everyone crazy. No matter how many times Otis said, "You know, doves are traditionally symbols of hope and peace," the children wanted to throttle it. Andrew and Luisa took it with them when they left. It hurt everyone to admit that they were abandoning something they had resolved to keep safe, but there wasn't any other choice.

There is no way to emerge subtly from behind a curtain of water. You can stick a hand through and hope no one notices, but then the water falls like bricks down onto your arm, and you have to get your arm out of there or lose it, so you either draw back or push through in a rush. Neither option is a good one, especially if you're hiding from a pack of rabid grown-ups. Luisa and Andrew held their breath and pushed. They stepped out, sopping wet, into the light. And thank God—they were alone. It was as though the island held no one but the two of them. And the dove. Which started warbling deep in the back of its throat immediately.

"Shh!" Andrew hissed, but the dove turned its head and cooed three times, loud.

"If you're not quiet, we'll throw you back in the cave," Luisa said. It was an empty threat. Everyone left in the cave would throw it right back out. Luisa and Andrew knew it, and the dove seemed to know it too. So the dove came with them, acting like a beacon, projecting their location.

Luisa and Andrew's feet were so callused from years of running barefoot that even when they stepped on thorns, the thorns didn't pierce their skin. They walked as quietly as they could. They stepped firmly on loose rocks, and the rocks stayed in place instead of moving suddenly to twist their ankles. Luisa thought she might have finally outgrown her childhood clumsiness. Only the sun, beating down on their heads, got to them, but they crouched in whatever shade they could find and drank in the temporary shadows as if they were water.

They weren't familiar with this part of the island. That there was a waterfall on the island at all had surprised them when they'd first found it. They'd been in such a panic that they hadn't registered the surprise, but still, from an outside distance, looking at it again, it didn't quite fit. Too tropical, somehow. Their island was an island of white crumbling stone and bougainvillea. The wildlife, rarely, if ever, seen, was goats. The flowers were bright, but tough, pulling water from dry earth. Their hut was whitewashed and baked by the sun. There was nothing lush about their world, usually. But now, looking back at the water that rushed down to conceal the entrance to the cave, Luisa thought they could easily be somewhere else entirely, a place with large-leafed dark green vegetation and flowers as big as her head. Was she seeing the world clearly? Had her eyes somehow corrected themselves, too?

When paired with the lush background, the dove's cooing sounded like the squawks of some tropical bird. Only her taupe feathers reminded Luisa of who she was.

"Let's get rid of her first," Luisa whispered.

Andrew nodded.

Luisa set off leading them, first on a path that took them away from the waterfall, and then on a path that twisted down closer to the sea. They both watched for the landscape to change, and it did, relatively quickly. They both kept their ears open for sounds of grown-ups, and they both jumped each time the dove made a noise. Neither of them thought it was a coincidence when the dove let out a particularly loud and full-throated warble at exactly the same time one of the grown-ups let out a loud, whinnying laugh. They thought it must have been the redhead, but which redhead? The one with the pink lipstick, or the one with the three inch heels? Or were they the same person? All those grown-ups blended together into one cruel mass, and Luisa thought that at least her vision of them, anyway, was accurate. It didn't matter which of those grown-ups was which. What mattered was how sharp their knives were and what they were planning to do with them. What mattered was that the dove was making noise and that hope was betraying them again.

Andrew shoved the bird beneath a bush. The dove looked at him reproachfully, then turned and waddled away. If she were a goddess, they'd abandoned her—they'd certainly failed some kind of test. But why should they think she was a goddess? What place was there for gods on that island? What place was there for hope of any kind? There were no gods. The entire world was on its own, the island most of all. The dove walked away, and, if anything, Luisa and Andrew felt free.

Or they would have felt free if there were no grown-ups to contend with. The redhead didn't seem to have heard the bird. Her own laugh must have deafened her. But she was close by, and they could hear her talking. And was that low grinding noise the sound of a knife being sharpened against a stone?

"The garbage is disgusting," they heard. "Think about what it's doing to our property value. We've got to get those kids back. Last night I tripped over a picture of my own mother. I had to throw it to the pigs myself."

"No!"

"Yes—and I cut myself on the broken glass."

"You poor thing."

"I know. I think those pigs thought I was part of the garbage. They started smacking their lips as soon as I got close. It's all that Eddie's fault. He told us to kill the spotted one. He forced us all to eat too much. I can barely fit into my pants."

"Me too. And let's not even talk about the hangover."

"It figures that Eddie would disappear. He arrives, we take him in, he causes trouble, and then he vanishes. Why should we be surprised? He had a terrible sense of style, anyway."

"We've got to get the children back. I don't care what it takes. I'm ready to get serious about hunting, even if it means I have to change my shoes. They're simply not allowed to disappear like this. They smell terrible, but the world smells even worse without them."

"If you're in, I'm in!"

"We'll pack a picnic. It might even be fun. At least it will get us away from the garbage."

The grown-ups' voices faded then. Andrew let out his breath. He hadn't realized he'd been holding it. He became aware, suddenly, that he was holding Luisa's hand, and realized he'd been holding it a lot lately. He let go of it, too.

"Come on," Luisa whispered. "Food. Before they turn around and find us. We're going to be hiding for a long time."

Andrew nodded. He shivered. He stepped in front of her and started down the overgrown path.

They walked for what seemed like hours. They avoided brambles. They didn't twist their ankles. A silent step here. A silent step there. It was real—everything was real. The island might have felt like a dream, but a pig had been speared and roasted and gobbled up until it was nothing but bones and Otis was in the cave without eyes. They each whispered inside their head that they were safe, trying as hard as they could to make that thought cover up all the other thoughts they had, which in Luisa were cold thoughts of resolution and in Andrew were black thoughts of dread, and in both were thoughts of fear so strong that their whole bodies shook.

The ocean was angry. They could see that as soon as they emerged from the wilderness above their hut. It was heaving and crashing, and each time it hit the shore it felt as if the entire shoreline shook. The pigs were hungry, hungry to a frenzy. They pushed themselves against the fence over and over and over. Maybe it was the pigs shoving that made the earth feel like it was shaking, not the ocean. Or maybe it was a combination of the two. Assault from all sides. And the garbage. They'd never seen garbage like this before. It crowded onto the sand, twenty feet thick extending out into the water. From a distance, it looked like dirty foam on the water's surface, but each step they took let them look more closely. Soon the trash separated into pieces until they could only think of it in parts, part upon part upon part without end. The water smacked the shore and the garbage pulsed and throbbed and the pigs howled and Luisa and Andrew stepped into a storm of agitation and fury.

There were Styrofoam coolers. There were rusty cake pans. There were bottles and bottles of half-used nail polish. There were cushions with holes from cigarette burns. There were paper plates. There were out-of-date computers still filled with personal data. There were onesies and toddler's outfits and little boy's pants with grass-stained knees. There were after-school art projects and handmade sweaters and Tupperware containers without lids. There were old people and sick people and middle-aged first wives. There were disabled war veterans. There were whole school buses full of children who crossed the border with nothing but knock-off Hello Kitty backpacks and faces wet with tears. The refuse extended like a road into the sea. The water shrugged and shrugged and tried to get away, but no matter how much it tried to shoulder the discards onto shore, more kept coming: the harvest was endless but the storehouse of the island wasn't big enough to hold it. The pigs threw themselves against the fence. They needed to eat, they were starving, they had work to do, but there was no one there to feed them.

There was something else, too. The smell. The air, just days before scented with thyme and lavender, with the bracing salt from the sea, and, most recently, the fragrance of roasting pig, smelled entirely rotten now. Molding chicken wings. Melon rind. Melted rubber. Even if the garbage hadn't massed on top of everything beautiful, the smell would have made the beauty impossible to see.

"There's got to be food here somewhere," Luisa said. Everything was clearer now than it had ever been. "Look at all this waste. There's probably enough buried in this trash to feed us for a year."

"I'm not going down there," Andrew said. "Look at what's being thrown away now."

Down at the ocean, a glacier nudged on shore, oozing water from its ice as if it were oozing tears.

"We're hungry," Luisa said. "It's awful, but we have to eat."

"It's not for us," Andrew said. "Remember Eddie? Remember that turkey sandwich? We feed it to the pigs. Rules are rules. We don't break them."

"Who says?" Luisa said. "Who sets up the rules? The pigs can't eat it all, anyway. There aren't enough of them left. Look at them—they can't even reach the garbage."

It was true. The pigs stared at the garbage, and the garbage massed as high as the children were tall, but there was a gap between where it massed and where the pigs paced behind the fence. All the pigs could do was gnash their teeth and occasionally bang against the fence and watch the food they lived on collect just a little ways away. It looked like hunger had roused them from their grief. It looked like their state right now was hunger without any possibility for satisfaction.

"Come on," Luisa said. "Ignore the pigs. Let's get food before the grown-ups come back." She ran down the hill. Andrew looked around. His stomach growled. He was starving. He shrugged and followed her.

And she was right. Beneath every third pile of rotting garbage, behind every distraught child and every forgotten great aunt and every piece of dying planet, there was something that was easy to swallow. The first thing he found was a stale half-eaten piece of chocolate cake. Someone must have ordered it before discovering they were just too full to finish. It was totally worth eating—he ate around the bite marks, and it was easy to forget that they were there. The second thing he found was a box of cereal that had been thrown away unopened. Its expiration date was past, but there was nothing wrong with it. It probably could have stood on a shelf forever and still been good. Andrew sat down among piles of garbage and ate handful after handful of sugared oats. Luisa sat beside him eating from a half-empty jar of pickles. Did pickles ever go bad? She didn't think they did. These were bright yellow, but they tasted delicious, even if the air all around them smelled terrible.

The garbage they were sitting in was piled so high that they couldn't see the pigs. They could hear them, though. Behind the garbage, behind the fence, the pigs shuffled back and forth, grunting in what sounded either like frustration or like panic, flinging themselves against the fence constantly, each time landing with a loud thud. They wanted to save the world, they really did. Their mouths were open and their stomachs were empty. There were only five now, but they were ready to try. But the pieces of the world couldn't get it together to be saved. They couldn't get it together to make it far enough for what amounted to a universal disposal system to dispose of them. They festered on the beach. And the pickings were plentiful and good.

Luisa drank a bright blue Gatorade that had been thrown away unopened.

Andrew rummaged through a backpack on a little girl's back and found a picture of her parents.

Luisa found immigration papers in a young man's wallet and ripped them up, throwing the pieces in the air so they rained down like confetti.

Andrew tried lasagna. He'd never had lasagna before, and he thought he could eat it forever. The grandmother who had cooked it without realizing her son's family no lon-

ger ate wheat stared at him and cried, but he just turned
his back and kept on eating. He'd never tasted anything as
good in his entire life.

The two of them were so full and had worked so hard to
ignore the smell and to forget that they should be gathering supplies to take back to the cave that they didn't hear it
when the grown-ups crept up behind them.

Long fingers closed around their necks. Long nails
strafed their skin. They were jerked to standing, and they
each felt what must have been knives poking into their backs.

"We're ready to gut you," a deep voice whispered. "We're
ready to string you up."

"Get to work," a voice like velvet crooned.

"We'll truss you like a chicken and roast you over a fire,"
a shrill voice hissed.

"Start cleaning," the velvet voice said. "Clean it all up and
feed it to the pigs."

"All of it," the deep voice said. "Clean it all up and maybe
we'll let you live."

There were five grown-ups surrounding them. They
moved in a cloud of cologne, but the cologne made all the
smells of garbage worse. They crossed their gloved arms
across their chests and kicked the children. The children
bent down slowly to pick up armfuls of trash. The grown-
ups shepherded the children from trash to pigs and back
again, nudging them as close to the pigs as they needed to
get in order to deposit the trash over the fence, and sometimes closer than was necessary. The pigs bared their teeth
and rolled their eyes and opened their mouths and gulped
down garbage. Luisa could feel their hot breath on her skin:
it was hotter than the day, even though it had become a very
hot day and the sun was doing its best to make the already

unbearable smell of garbage even more unbearable. From somewhere inside the garbage heap an old woman cried.

"We're going to find the others," the velvet voice whispered. It came from the mouth of a grown-up with long blonde hair, and when she leaned in close her hair got caught in her teeth. "You're going to clean up this mess, then you're going to lead us to them, and then they're going to come back and do the work they're supposed to do until another shipment of children arrives. Then we'll feed you all to the pigs. You've done a terrible job, but you're going to keep doing it. Move faster."

She slipped her foot out of her shoe and picked it up and hit Luisa across the head with its heel.

The heel was sharp. It tore Luisa's skin. She crouched down and wiped blood away from her eyes. Her hand curled into a fist.

"We're not telling you where they are," Andrew said.

A man with light brown hair plastered flat across his balding head slipped a belt out of his pants and snapped it in the air.

The pigs threw themselves against the fence and mashed their jaws open and shut.

The belt snapped hard against Andrew's calves. He yelped and bent down and pressed his hands where it had hit him. The belt snapped again, this time against his hand. He pulled his hand away and stuck his fingers in his mouth. The pigs grunted. The man laughed.

"Move," a third woman said. Her fingers dripped with emeralds and her eyelash extensions fluttered against her cheeks. She pressed her face close to Luisa's face. "Move, or we'll drop you over the fence and get rid of you right now. We wouldn't mind watching you eaten piece by piece."

"I'd actually love to see that," the brown-haired man said.

"Me too," the blonde said. "Maybe we could just do it now?"

"The garbage," the third woman said, pinching her nose with willowy fingers. "After the garbage." She handed Luisa an empty trash bag. Luisa stuffed it full of anything her hands could reach: stuffed animals in need of repair; mouth guards covered with plaque; wool sweaters run through the dryer; chipped asbestos tiles; a homeless man with dementia; a housewife with no husband, no career, and children who'd grown up and moved to cities far away. She shoved them in the bag. She lugged the bag over the rough ground, heaved it over the fence, and stepped back to watch the pigs swallow its contents down. They chewed fast and hard, like they'd skipped ahead in the stages of grief and settled for now on anger. They were merciless, and Luisa could tell that they made no distinction between the children who fed them and the torturers who pushed them to it and the trash that they consumed between their snapping jaws. Maybe there was really no distinction to be made.

Day faded into night. Tears turned into hiccups into silence. From a distance, the island settled down. A ship steamed toward the horizon. It rode low in the water, heavy with all its baggage, looking forward to dawn when it would drop its trash and steam on, buoyant, so light in the water that it might as well have been flying.

Back at the cave, Eddie woke from sleeping with a gasp, shouting that something had gone wrong. He wouldn't quiet down until they all agreed to take a look. It was blackest night when they emerged, Otis and Eddie and Mimi and Natasha. The waterfall parted like a curtain to let each one through, and washed each in its gap so they were sparkling when they stepped onto the path. The water's coldness forced their eyes wide open. They could see the varying shapes of shadows even if they couldn't see what cast them.

All of them except Otis. He didn't care about eyes opening anymore. He cared about sound.

The night was filled with odd noises. Owls hooting. A dove in deep mourning. The ocean gurgling as if gasping for air.

In the distance, far below, lights moved in strange trajectories, lanterns dangling from the disaffected wrists of wardens. Beyond the lanterns, the ocean looked white. On a stormy night, under a full moon, the white might have been foam, but it was a calm night, there was no moon, and the white could only be trash. The island shrugged. The sea moaned. They could hear cries in the far distance. It sounded like someone was in deep pain. They held onto each other for comfort and stumbled on the path in the dark.

Only Otis, who couldn't see, walked without difficulty, and because he kept walking, the rest followed him, trusting that he'd lead them along the path, taking three steps for his every one to keep up.

"What do we do if they catch us?" Mimi whispered. She was holding tight to Natasha's hand and looked tired enough to be a mother. Natasha wriggled away from her, or tried to, but Mimi wouldn't let go. "What do we do if they put us in a net?"

"Put sharp rocks in your pocket," Eddie said. "Sharp enough to saw through rope." Mimi couldn't see him in the dark, but his voice made her trust him. "If they catch us, pretend to struggle, but don't struggle too much. When you're in the net, start sawing. They won't be able to see it in the dark. Then, when we're all out, we slip back to the cave."

"No one gets left behind," Mimi said.

"Of course," Eddie said.

"What's happening?" Natasha said.

"Sharp rocks," Eddie said. "Find sharp rocks."

Mimi stooped down to find rocks with edges and pulled Natasha down beside her. Otis kept walking. Eddie hissed at him to slow down, and he tried, but it was as though once he started going he couldn't stop on his own. Forward, forward, forward—his legs kept moving, and every time he took a step they had to run to catch up.

At times the lanterns the grown-ups carried looked like stars fallen down to earth. They pinpointed their location, so they were useful to the children watching, but they were beautiful, too. Fire contained in a glass box: light for the world, even in overwhelming darkness. Watching the signs of the grown-ups was like watching stars moving off arcs that spoke of harmony. It was a confirmation that desire undermined the order of the world, and that beauty and order were not always partners.

Otis, maybe because he was blind, was not disoriented by the darkness in the same way the children were. He walked quickly, and he never stumbled. He didn't seem to need to grope at bushes with his hands. When the path turned, he turned. When the path jogged downhill, he slowed his pace just a tiny bit so he wasn't caught off guard. Unlike the children, he wasn't distracted by the lights. Without sight, he walked with a singleness of purpose. Mimi wanted to ask him what he was walking toward, but she couldn't catch up with him. Each time she sped up and was almost by his side, dragging Natasha with her, he sped up too, rushing forward, moving toward the sea.

"Wait, Otis," she called out, but not too loud—there were grown-ups down below. "Wait for us."

He kept walking. He pulled so far ahead of them that, given that there was no moon, it was a miracle they could see him at all.

"We need to make a plan," she called. But it was a whispered call, the kind that was carried by the force of breath, not by the level of sound made. He didn't seem to hear.

"Don't get too far ahead," she said, as loud as she dared. And then he *did* get too far ahead, and whatever miracle was making it possible for her to see him in the dark lost its power. He stepped over a rock and vanished. The pigs squealed, far away.

Mimi and Eddie and Natasha pressed close together and trudged on without a guide. They kept expecting to catch up with Otis. But each time they turned a curve in the path, he must have turned a new one. And without his back to keep their eyes on, without any warning about the pitfalls on the path, they stumbled each time they came to one. A rock? They turned their ankles. A narrowing in of pricker bushes? They got pricked. A quick turn? They kept walking straight, with all the perils that entailed. They were scratched and bruised and sore, and the sharp-edged rocks in their pockets were heavy. The night wasn't turning out well, for all the beauty they'd had by way of consolation.

And then they felt a whip snap out of the dark and wrap around their waists. It was the kind of whip a lion tamer uses to rope and herd and lock wild beasts back inside of cages. "We've got you," a voice sang out of the darkness. "We've got you all together. You're ours now, until the end."

Otis could hear the children behind him. They stumbled on every root like their eyes were good for nothing. He heard Mimi's hissing call to slow down. He heard a knock, and whimpering that must have come from Eddie. None of the other children would whimper. He'd begun to know them well by sound. They each had a distinct way of breathing. They each had a distinct footfall. The feel of their hands was different when they took him by the arm to guide him through rough terrain. They were kind. They cared for him, broken though he was. He walked on ahead of them. The world, in its darkness, was intimate. He took sure step after sure step, and he didn't think about the fact that each step widened the gap between him and the children.

Children. He couldn't stop thinking about his own son. He would be almost Andrew's age. Or Luisa's age. Not as young as Natasha, but still young enough to hold his father's hand when they crossed a city street. When he'd last said goodbye to Alice, she'd kissed him. It was a hurried kiss, for show, mostly. She had other things on her mind besides saying goodbye. The phone was ringing. Something was baking in the oven. She had a babysitter scheduled and plans to go out that night. They said when he returned they'd try a reconciliation but he knew her heart wasn't really in it. He could feel her mind sliding off somewhere sideways when her lips met his, and at other times this would have sparked a fight, but at that moment his mind was traveling too.

Every time he left home, he left because he couldn't bear to stay. The sea was wide open ahead and life in the house shrunk narrower and narrower. He left when it got too tight to breathe.

But his son. He'd tried so hard to keep his mind on him, to be present whenever he was near. When he'd pressed his hands into his son's thin back, he could feel every knuckle of his spine. The kid was so skinny. He must have grown overnight that last time he'd hugged him. Otis hadn't been away from him for more than eight hours while he slept, and already he was taller. Already he looked like he knew something about the world he hadn't known the night before. That skinny kid was the thing that made it hard to leave.

"I'm here with you," Otis had whispered.

"Not for long," his son had said.

"I'll be back." It had been hard for Otis not to cry just then.

"I know," his son had said. "You always come back. I just don't know how long it will be until you do."

"Not too long," Otis said.

"Promise," his son had said.

"I promise."

What a liar I am, he thought. There was no way he was going back now. Look where he'd ended up. Or don't look, that was impossible now—feel. The earth made itself known beneath his feet, but he couldn't see. How would he recognize his own son when he came running down the path to greet him? People change. Voices change. What was certain once is never certain again. How would his son recognize him?

He knew he was kidding himself. His eyes had nothing to do with whether or not he'd recognize his own child.

The problem was that, having spent time on the island, he'd started thinking about all the children there as his children. Andrew was the sweetest. That boy needed a father so badly you could smell it on his skin. Mimi was almost a woman, and the change from girl to woman was a hard transition to make. He wanted to be there for those moments when she still needed a parent. Luisa would be a leader someday. He was reserving his judgment on Natasha, but there was a chance she'd turn out all right. Children straightened themselves out all the time. Even Eddie had the potential to change. He could sense potential in them both. The trick was to get them to see it in themselves.

The children on the island had no one. They needed him.

He walked on, and didn't hear when the whip cracked around the children he was in the process of leaving behind.

Otis could feel the air stretching out around him. It was cold, but it would be hot when the sun came up. He had left the narrow path, and the island opened up as he neared the sea. The pigs were to his right. The water lay straight ahead. He could smell its salt beneath the rotten stench that seeped through every spare part of the world. There was a soft crying over by the water. Probably Andrew and Luisa. Probably tired and in need of some sleep.

Otis's feet felt the change from earth to plastic without warning. One minute his callused soles were on cool stone and crumbling dirt. The next, he'd stepped on the edge of a yogurt container and cut his foot. It was a silly way to cut himself. The container had ripped on its journey and its edge was thin and jagged. He howled before he realized he was making noise.

The whole island must have heard him, because when he stopped, he thought he heard the dove mimicking his cries from somewhere behind him in the brush.

He expected one of the children to run to him and help him find a bandage, but then he remembered that he'd rushed ahead—though he couldn't remember why—and that he was the one who should take care of them. And part of taking care of them was not allowing them to do the same for him in return. Why was he always rushing? Why did he never turn back until it was too late?

He lifted his foot to his hand to check the damage. His balance was perfect, and in the dark with no one watching he looked like a crane. His fingers came back from the sole of his foot sticky with blood. He rubbed his hand clean on his thigh. He had to keep going. His foot hurt, but he would put it in the water. Saltwater was good for cleaning cuts. He wasn't scared. That water wouldn't be able to add anything to the grief he already felt.

He stepped more carefully now. It turned out someone had bought an entire case of yogurts and had thrown them all away unopened. He imagined they'd bought them to pack for lunches. Maybe a child got sick, and couldn't go to school. Or maybe they'd bought them to take to the office after a New Year's resolution to lose weight, but then got tired of eating yogurt every day. Maybe they'd just forgotten about the containers in the back of the refrigerator until their expiration dates announced that they'd gone bad. Who knows why yogurt gets thrown away in such vast quantities? You'd think it would be enough to buy one or two containers at a time.

When his son was small, he'd been allergic to cow's milk. His stomach had puffed up oddly, and he'd held his little legs to his chest and cried after he had ice cream. It was impossible to find anything made with goat's milk, even in the health food section of the store. Alice bought a yogurt maker, and raw goat's milk from a hippie who owned goats a couple of towns away, and turned their kitchen into a hospitable place for bacteria. The yogurt she produced was sour and thin. They mixed it with strawberry jam, but even they, adults with knowledge of the work that had gone into it and the health problems it might solve, winced when they put it in their mouths. Their son howled and clamped his mouth shut whenever a spoon came near.

"It's sweet," they'd said. "Just try a bite."

He shook his head and kicked his legs. Maybe he remembered his stomachaches from other forms of dairy. Maybe he was smart enough to tell when his parents were lying.

I hope not, Otis had thought. *Please let him be a little older before he knows I've lied to him.*

At any rate, they were stuck with a new yogurt maker to throw away, bottles of goats milk in the refrigerator, and a batch of yogurt nobody wanted to eat.

Smart son, he'd thought. *Get your calcium from greens. Don't let anyone force you to eat something you don't like.*

He remembered Alice crying with frustration. "Everything hurts his stomach," she'd said. "How can I keep him alive if he won't eat anything?"

"He'll be fine," Otis had said, but even as he'd said it, he himself couldn't tell if he believed what he was saying or not.

He wondered if that yogurt maker was here, kicking itself against the coast.

He was limping now. He could hear the pigs shuffling back and forth close by. He thought he'd wash his feet in the water, then double back and bring them a treat in their pen. There was so much here they'd like. He could feel it beneath his feet, and he could smell it, and he could hear the way the waves worked to heave it onto land. Maybe he'd start with the yogurt containers, in honor of his son. He could move from there to instructions for taking antibiotics, and maybe after that the pigs might like the worn out sneakers that were clogging up the path. His stomach growled. He was hungry. He wished he could eat some of this stuff— he wondered what differences, beyond texture, colored each separate piece of refuse.

The air felt different. Warmer at its edges. He guessed that the sun was coming up, that the day was on the rise. He wondered what he looked like to the children. He still thought about the world in visual terms, and he wondered when that would fade. For now, he pictured himself from behind. He was dressed in rags. He limped when he walked. His arms and legs were hard with muscles, but skinny. His thigh was smeared with blood. They might not think he was the man to save them. They might not want him around to witness them grow up.

But what could he do? Was there really any other choice?

The pigs whistled.

He felt the water kiss his feet.

The grown-ups laughed so loud that it sounded like they were shrieking, and their shrieking rose above the waves.

Otis nodded. He bent down and scooped up an armful of trash. It was unwieldy, but it wasn't heavy. He took as much as his arms could hold and turned around and stumbled toward the pigs.

The grown-ups laughed, and it looked like Otis didn't hear them—who could hear them with the ocean struggling to push the glacier onto shore? The ice cracked so loudly that it covered over every other sound in the entire world. The ice melted and the water level rose and the ocean heaved and heaved and the ground on which the garbage collected grew smaller which just made the amounts of trash look bigger, and Otis kept on walking.

The dawn shone pink around the outline of his body. Old shoes fell from his arms. The pigs rushed back and forth, licking their lips. The grown-up with emeralds on her fingers shoved her hand into Luisa's back and Luisa knocked into Andrew and Andrew knocked into Eddie—everyone was tied together now, the children from the path, the children from the pen, the thrown-out humans washed ashore, the old, the young, the dying, the abandoned, the cast-aside, the forgotten. And there was Otis. Walking straight into a trap.

"Get him," the deep-voiced grown-up said. "Shove him into the pen. He's too pathetic to keep."

"I'll do it," the red-haired woman said. She'd come down the hill with Natasha and Eddie and Mimi wrapped in a whip in front of her. Her heels made her wobble, but she held on tight to her cigarette holder and moved it with enough control to flick ashes onto Mimi's skin.

"Otis," Andrew screamed. The glacier thundered. His voice was lost.

Otis kept walking toward them, smiling, lifting his face to the sun. Blood trailed behind him. He didn't seem to care.

"Shh," Eddie hissed.

Andrew looked at him. Eddie's arms were pressed against his body, but his hands were working at something, and, slowly, he managed to pry a sharp edged stone from his pocket. He handed it to Andrew and reached back in for another. The two boys nodded. Then they sawed at each other's ropes. Mimi turned her head and saw them. She opened her eyes wide, remembering the stones she'd placed in her own pockets. She managed to get two out, and pushed one into Luisa's palm. The crashing ice and the sobs of refugees masked the sawing sounds. Otis, trash falling from his over-full arms, stole any focus from the children, and they sawed their ropes through without attracting notice. Only Natasha's hands were still bound. She was mumbling something about planning a spa weekend, and it didn't seem worth asking her to help.

The grown-ups left the tied-up children behind and sneaked up to Otis as stealthily as they could. They took long steps, but crouched low to the ground, thrusting out their legs, pressing their fingers against their lips. One of them wore an anklet that was made of diamonds. The sun caught the stones and reflected so bright that only a blind man wouldn't see the sparkle. Luckily for them, Otis was blind.

The sharp-edged rocks worked. The cord snapped in two. Andrew pushed the ropes down from his arms, down from his chest, into a pile of frayed twine at his feet. He stepped free. Luisa did the same. Mimi brushed hair off Natasha's face and whispered as quietly as she could that they would come back for her, that she wasn't really being left alone, that she wasn't lost forever.

"Take me to the races," Natasha said. "I've heard mint juleps are delicious."

A man with a walrus mustache loomed just inches away from Otis, and it seemed crazy that Otis didn't notice the danger. Couldn't he smell the man? The children could smell the cologne from even where they stood. But Otis just walked on, his arms overflowing, his face marked by blood and tears and mud that the waterfall had missed, his body hobbled by twisted ankles and long scratches and bruises that had no clear source of origin. The pigs were practically howling. Otis just kept saying, "Don't worry, I'm coming, I'll take care of you." He stepped forward, and just as he did, the mustachioed man reached his beefy hands out and pushed him hard.

And that was it. Who knew that Otis could move quickly? He twisted and pushed his overflowing arms at the man and garbage shifted from him to the grown-up and with his empty hands he grabbed the man and wouldn't let go.

"We're both going over," he said. "I'm not letting you hurt those children anymore." They lurched into the fence. Otis folded himself at the waist, the man on top of him, garbage spilling out around them, Otis's hands holding onto thick, muscly flesh. And then something gave, and then air opened up beneath him, and then the two toppled together, head first into the pigpen. They landed together on hard earth.

The pigs froze. The world froze. For a moment, all that existed was Otis on the ground, and the pigs staring at him with mouths wide open, and the man scrambling back to the fence. And then the pigs lunged.

But they didn't lunge at Otis. They lunged at the man, and, while Otis lay there breathless, listening to the world come close, the pigs began their work.

It was horrible, really. There were only five pigs left, and they took their time, but there was no question about whether they were up to the job. They started at the lower end: first feet, clad in tasseled loafers, and then legs, fatty and thick with hair. They teased the cummerbund off the waist, and popped each button off the jacket, and gobbled up the necktie like they'd never tried necktie before. The mustache seemed to give them some problems—maybe the wiry hairs caught in their throats. But once they'd coughed a few times, they were eager to finish up, and before anyone knew it, the man was gone. Vanished. Like he'd never existed at all.

Otis moved to the side, surrounded by garbage, shaking. He'd made a choice. At last. He thought he'd made the right one, but it didn't mean they wouldn't eat him, too. He might have made the choice too late. He might deserve to disappear. He put his hand out. He felt the warm bristly back of a pig. She was crouched on her haunches and he thought she must be looking through the fence, she and her sisters, like a dog trusting that another reward was on its way. He pushed his cheek against her flank. He stroked his hand up and down. She nestled into it. He patted her and sighed.

Luisa grabbed the red-haired woman and led her to the fence. The woman seemed stunned, and she walked without making a fuss. Maybe she was in shock. Maybe so much had changed in that moment about what she understood the rules of the world to be that she couldn't gather her thoughts together enough to resist. It wasn't until she was right at the slats that she seemed to wake up and realize where she was being led. She struggled. She twisted and scratched and screamed and kicked, but she was no match once the other children moved in to help. She fell over the fence with her long hair streaming, and within a few minutes, all that was left of her was a string of pearls. One of the pigs stuck her head through the necklace and sat back with it dangling against her belly. The other pigs seemed to laugh. They had a little blood around their mouths, but beyond that they might as well have been eating slop.

The blonde with the emeralds put up the biggest fight. She used her long nails to scratch and her sharp teeth to bite, and by the time they got her over the fence, the children's arms were bleeding and their faces had little chunks torn out. But they worked together. She toppled over the fence just like the others. Otis patted the pigs and whispered to them to go at it. The pigs seemed to enjoy the fight. They burped when they were done, and then opened their mouths and smiled and waited expectantly for the rest of their meal.

Amazingly, after years of persecution, it took almost no time to feed the entire passel of grown-ups to the pigs. Once the children realized they could seize the moment and work together, the grown-ups slipped easily into the pigs' open mouths. The blonde with the comb over disappeared silently. The black-haired man with the streak of white like lightning groaned during his entire passage down the pigs' long throats. Women in tight dresses and men in tuxedoes vanished, screaming. It was painful being eaten. It was painful letting go of the world.

And then the pigs were quiet. The island was quiet, too, except for the laments of various pieces of detritus, and except for Natasha's chatter. She looked almost as old as the grown-ups by then, and she stayed clear of the pen as if by instinct. "I'm so lonely," she whispered. "The only thing that will make me feel better is a slice of chocolate cake." The other children looked at one another. They still had sharp rocks in their hands. They could kill her quickly, give her a sudden, easily marked death instead of one that was carried out bite by bite. But silent communication failed them, and they pretended not to notice when she slunk away.

From a distance, the screams of grown-ups echoed in the entire world's ears. From a distance, the noise sounded like another chainsaw cutting down another old-growth tree. Help wanted ads went out across the world. It didn't take long for lines of job applicants to circle every single city block they could.

Everyone looked at Otis. His beat-up hands with their thick knuckles and scabby wrists reached out to scratch the top of the skinny pig's head, to straighten out the thin pink ear of the one with dainty hooves, to cup the sharp-toothed one under the chin, to adjust the pearls that dangled from the neck of the pig with the itchy back. He whispered something to them, and they kept their attention on his words and looked at him silently and with adoration.

"I had a family once," he said.

"We've heard this story before," Luisa whispered. "Doesn't he have any new ones?"

"Shh," Andrew said.

"We lived by the shore. I had a wife and a child and a house and a backyard. I had a job. It took me away for months at a time, but it was the only job I was suited for.

"Or maybe I've got it wrong. I wanted to leave. I was afraid of the way my wife and my child shot roots through my heart. It was only when I was traveling that I knew for certain that I wanted to be home. As soon as I got home I wanted to ship out again. I have a restless heart."

Mimi sighed. If it had been a few days ago, she might have rolled her eyes, but she was older now, and more than anything, she was tired. Luisa could feel how heavy her head was where it rested on her shoulder. She reached her arm out and circled it around Mimi's waist. Mimi let her head rest heavier, let Luisa support her entire body on her shoulder.

The dove warbled softly.

"At any rate, I ran away." Otis was speaking to the pigs, but his voice had risen, and now it filled the entire island. It was very loud. "The sea was a strange place to become a man. I learned about the world as a place you sail by, as a place you stop in temporarily. The ship was constant. Land was as liquid as water. I know I had a child at some point. I remember holding him in my arms. I know I had a wife as well but, honestly, I can't remember what she looked like. I think her hair was brown. I think she sunburned easily. I think she liked to sing, but when I try to hear her voice I can only hear my own."

The sun rose above the sea. The water reflected clouds. Luisa looked hard—were those cloud shapes on the water really a reflection? They somehow looked too solid. She trusted herself. She could see things that others couldn't see. She took Mimi's elbow and she took Eddie's hand, and she pulled them with her toward the water.

"Do you think my son remembers me?" Otis said. "Do you think he's forgiven me for leaving?"

The pigs batted their eyes at Otis. The sun turned their bristly skin pink. The blood on their cheeks looked like rouge.

"I can't return to him now. I can't return to the world. I haven't given it anything that would make it take me back."

They weren't reflections. The sea was paved with old refrigerators. They floated on the water like giant tiles. Somewhere back on earth they'd been replaced by stainless steel Sub-Zeros, and here, on the water, the discarded refrigerators were white. The large white tiles stretched out forever until vision failed.

"I can't see a thing," Otis said. "I used to love through my eyes, but that's impossible now. And you know what? I don't even miss it. It's crazy, but, without eyes, crying is a totally different thing. And maybe more than that: without eyes I can shape the world how I want it, in my head. I don't have to look at the things I don't want to see."

Luisa shook her head. He was wrong—what crept into her vision when her eyes were shut was more unwanted than anything she saw when she opened them. A brother in a net. A man with blood dripping from his empty sockets. A high-heeled foot disappearing down the throat of an enormous pig. But who was she to tell him he was wrong? Maybe things were different for different people. Those refrigerators looked like a path to her. Other people might not be able to see it, but she was pretty sure she could actually step onto them and follow them out forever.

"You children should go," Otis said. "Just go. I want to stay here with the pigs. I'll tend to them. They love me."

Eddie's grip on Luisa's hand tightened. She looked at him, and for the first time she could match his expression to the worry in her heart.

Andrew was standing next to Mimi now. His arm was wrapped around her, and she looked old. She wore a shapeless dress. Her calves had thickened. Her hair looked as though it hadn't been washed in days, and as though the grit coating its tips was spit up baby food. She looked so tired. She looked as though, tired as she was, she'd stay awake all night to comfort a child with a fever. She reached into her pocket, drew out Otis's chain, and hooked it around her neck. His empty locket hit her heart. She shifted her weight to Andrew and he pulled her close.

Luisa let go of Eddie's hand. She walked to the pigpen, to reach across to Otis. She held her hands out in front of her, her eight fingers spread apart. He reached across the fence and hugged her to him. She'd spent a lifetime shuttling garbage from the sea to the pen, but she'd never looked closely at the way the pen was held together. Now, pressed against Otis's bony chest, she turned her head to the side and saw that a rusting lock fastened the post she stood at to the rest of the pen. It was a gate, and in all her life she'd never once thought about the pen having a gate.

"We can let them out," she said.

Eddie sucked in his breath.

She tugged at the lock, and it creaked but didn't move. She looked at the keyhole. It was large, like it was made for an old-fashioned key. The holes were just the size of her fingers.

"Don't," Andrew said. He pulled Mimi closer and put his other arm around Eddie's back.

"They can run wild," Luisa said. "They can eat whatever they want. We can all leave together."

The keyholes looked almost like the fingers of a glove. She looked at her hand. She pressed her lips together. She nodded once, and then nodded again, and then she shoved her left hand inside. When she pressed her thumb into the palm of her hand, the rest of her three fingers slid neatly into slots. Her pinky stub made all the difference. If she'd still had that extra finger, the space inside would have been too crowded. She turned her hand. The lock turned, too. Easily. Like it had been oiled every day for a thousand years just waiting for a kid to find meaning in injury. She pulled her hand out. She tugged at the gate. It moved. The pigs sighed together, like they'd been holding in their breath and could finally let it go.

"Go down to the water," Otis said. He reached his hands across to Luisa's shoulders. His voice was steady. "I'll wait until you're gone to open the pen."

"No," Luisa said. "We're not leaving you."

He leaned forward and pushed her hands away from the gate. His weight on the unlocked wood made it creak. The pigs pressed against it.

"Go now," he said.

The children looked at him. He didn't see them nod, but he felt their absence as soon as they moved away.

The children walked down to the water.

The pigs sat silent and watched them leave with their small eyes that hid what they were thinking.

"Just go," Otis called after them. "Walk out into the sea. Someone will come to rescue you." The rising sunlight filled his hands. He lifted it up, turned it over, and cast it down to the pigs, and the pigs sang.

They sang while the children stepped onto the garbage. They sang while the children jumped from one refrigerator to the next. The dove shifted on the branch and then opened her wings and flew out to sea in front of them, a swift-winged guide, a promise of hard-won, nagging hope. The children followed. The pigs' voices separated into a six part harmony that was as sweet as anything the children had ever heard, even if one of the lines of harmony was missing. Luisa looked back. Otis had pulled the unlatched gate wide open, and each pig—the one with the lopped off ear, the one whose hooves looked dainty, the one who liked to scratch her side against the fence post, the one who was smaller and skinnier than the rest but who seemed to have the sharpest teeth of all, and the one she always forgot to count—each pig stalked to the shore and sang to say goodbye. The path the children followed extended out forever, and behind them it disappeared: each pig ended her song and opened her mouth and prepared to swallow the discarded world whole.

News went out across the world. A freighter had rescued four children walking on a path of garbage across the sea. They were so traumatized by their experience that everything they said came out as nonsense. Where were their parents? Where had they been raised? Who lets children wander unsupervised across the ocean? They huddled together on board the ship, linked their hands together, and ate like they'd been starving their entire lives when the sailors thought to bring them food. And the world looked for someone to blame.

Beyond the finger-pointing, though, the world was worried. Ships weren't supposed to pick up trash. They were supposed to drop it in the water and sail on without looking back. What would happen to the garbage now?

But then, from a distance, sighs of relief were exhaled. Rumor had it that a new system was in place. Five pigs roamed freely and a swineherd put them to bed at night. The pigs, with a wider area to range in and all the possibility for exercise that the new territory held, worked up an enormous appetite, and when garbage arrived it almost didn't matter that there were only five pigs now instead of six. Life could keep on exactly as it always had—nobody paid attention to the garbage those five pigs simply didn't have room to digest.

When ships passed, they could sometimes hear a man's voice singing. Sometimes the voice sang lullabies. Sometimes the voice sang scraps of poems set to a kind of tuneless music. Sometimes the voice sang a single note that spread out, miraculously, into polyphonic harmony. Nobody cared who the singer was. Nobody cared how he split his voice into so many simultaneous notes. What they cared about was that the world maintained its order, and it did.

From a distance, the island was the tidiest place on earth, and each piece of garbage traveling across the water was guaranteed to find a home. It was a misunderstanding that anything was lost forever. It was a misunderstanding that anything ever really disappeared.

BIOGRAPHICAL NOTE

Johanna Stoberock is the author of the novel *City of Ghosts*. Her honors include the James W. Hall Prize for Fiction, an Artist Trust GAP award, and a Jack Straw Fellowship. In 2016, she was named runner-up for the Italo Calvino Prize for Fiction. Her work has appeared in the *New York Times*, the *Best of the Net* anthology, and *Catamaran*, among others. She lives in Walla Walla, Washington, where she teaches at Whitman College. www.johannastoberock.com